By H.A. Blackwood

Tell-Tale Hearts

Tell-Tale Hearts

HA Blackwood

Baying Hound's Dark Side

USA

Disclaimers and Copyright

This book is a work of fiction. Names, characters, places, and incidents are the product of the author's imagination or used fictitiously and are not to be construed as real. Any resemblance to actual persons, living or dead, locales, or events—no matter how sexy or erotic—is purely coincidental and not intended by the author.

This book is not suitable for an audience under the age of 18. It contains explicit sexual content, risky sexual behavior, dubious consent, and strong language.

TELL-TALE HEARTS

Copyright © 2019 by HA Blackwood
All rights reserved.
Published by Baying Hound's Dark Side
Edited by Amanda Blow

ISBN: 978-0-9988282-6-8

Thank you...

For reading this literal invention of my subconscious mind. I had a dream one night – vivid, sexual, explicit – and when I woke up, I remember thinking *"Whoa, that was intense!"* I promptly fell back asleep and I had the exact. Same. Dream. Scene for scene, act for act, it was identical.

When I awoke the second time, I took the hint my subconscious was clearly trying to deliver to me, and I made some notes. A month later, the first draft was done, and a month after that, the ebook was published.

I appreciate you taking the time to read this tale. I must tell you; it was fun to write. I hope it turns you on as much reading it as it did me when I was writing it. In any case, it's yours now. Enjoy!

- HAB

Gemma

I was halfway through a thirty-minute session on my treadmill when she walked over and got on one directly in front of mine. It couldn't be a coincidence—it was the third time this week she'd picked a treadmill in my direct line of sight. I had a tendency, especially lately, to be attracted to other women, so it wasn't surprising that she'd caught my eye. I just wasn't sure, until now, if she was trying to get my attention. Thinking she might just have a favorite machine that happened to be in front of mine, today I grabbed one way down the line from my usual spot, and sure enough, here she was. Her choice of placement had to be intentional.

Not that I minded. This woman was, in a word, *hot*. She wore tight running shorts and a sporty red top, cropped sleeves, tapered so her midriff showed just a hint as she ran. Her form was perfect. For grins, because I wasn't following the episode of *Judge Judy* on the TV in front of me, I counted her strides for thirty seconds. Forty-five, meaning her strides-per-minute totaled ninety. Perfect.

Her brown skin was a smooth cover over well-toned muscles. She looked like she was about five foot seven, and maybe one hundred twenty-five

1

pounds, and had, at a guess, C-cup breasts. Probably 34C, maybe 36B. She had silky, jet black hair that fell between her shoulders, held in check by an elastic hair-tie so her ponytail bobbed back and forth as she ran.

I leaned to one side to see what pace she had the treadmill set. She was running eight-minute miles—seven and a half miles per hour!—and had the countdown set for thirty minutes, though it was down to twenty-eight.

So, I knew that she was purposely positioning herself in front of me, essentially forcing me to look at her wonderful ass while she ran. I just didn't know why.

My five-foot eight-inch frame and 36Cs weren't anything to sneeze at, but I haven't had a woman be so... deliberate about putting herself on display for me. I wondered what her intentions were. I mean, she could be trying to pick me up, obviously, and that would be flattering if I weren't at the bottom of a deep emotional trough. I needed a "complicated doesn't begin to describe it" relationship status on Facebook. So, I thought I knew what she might be up to, but I wasn't going to make assumptions, especially after my last super passionate, but ill-advised affair crashed and burned. Clearly, the calibration on my judgment was off.

My thirty minutes were up, and even though there were a ton of machines open, I don't like to hog them for more than the requested time limit. If I needed to run for more than thirty minutes, I'd go outside and do it.

The gym had squirt bottles filled with cleaning solution stashed every thirty feet around the massive room, so I grabbed one and wiped the treadmill down. God forbid someone might get near some of my sweat! As far as I was concerned, that was the most innocent of bodily fluids.

As I walked to the free-weights area, I passed a heavyset man who was punishing another treadmill, his feet pounding on the tread, his breath coming hard and fast like a steam engine. I could see spittle blowing all over the console, and he was sweating like a cold glass of water on a hot, humid day. Maybe the spray bottles were a good idea, after all.

Today was my arms and shoulders day, so I did a circuit of curls, shoulder presses, front and lateral raises, and tricep presses. When I finished, I walked over to the area designated for stretching. I liked to get everything loose, especially my hamstrings, after a good workout. I had just sat down and gotten comfortable when I saw the woman headed my way. Something about her seemed very familiar, but I could not place her face. I expected her to pass by and get a drink from the water fountain, but she stopped in front of me.

Good god, she was pretty. She wore almost no makeup and was dewy with sweat, giving her a post-sex vibe. Her dark complexion matched her light brown eyes. I felt a familiar tingle as this brown-skinned goddess extended her right hand toward me.

"Hi! I'm Gemma Amante."

I reached up and took her hand. I didn't know if it was real or my imagination, but I felt a physical spark like she had walked across shag carpet instead of a rubber gym floor. I returned her smile. "I'm Darcy Ford."

She squatted down in front of me. "It's good to meet you, Darcy. I've meant to introduce myself for a week now. I've seen you here at the same time as me, mostly on the same days. You have good running form."

I smiled. "Well, I can't go seven-five for a half hour, but I get by."

A grin crept over her face. "So, you were checking out my settings?"

I blushed, realizing I'd exposed myself. Now Gemma knew I was watching her with more than a casual interest. If we were playing a game, I decided to turn the focus back to her, so I played offense. "Well, you keep parking yourself on a treadmill right in front of me. It's kind of hard not to notice you. Not for nothing, but you're much more fun to watch than afternoon TV."

She sat down, the sly grin spreading wider across her face. "It was that obvious? You probably think I'm a creep or something."

"No, you're..." I paused. I almost said too much.

"I'm what?"

"Nothing."

She reached out and slapped my foot. "Tell me! You *do* think I'm a creep!"

"No, you're perfect. That's what I was going to say, but I thought that would make *me* sound like a creep." I aped a caveman's speech pattern. "Me Darcy. See girl, say wrong thing. Scare away."

She laughed an easy laugh, heartfelt and honest. It made me want to laugh, too, so I did.

"You're sweet, thank you for saying that," she said. "It makes all the working out worthwhile, even if it's not true."

She was gracious and modest. I was starting to like her. "Well, I guess no one is perfect, but you're awfully close."

"Well, you're a fine specimen yourself, by the way. Hey, can you help me stretch? My hamstrings could really use it."

"You bet! I was just getting ready to work on mine when you came over."

She extended her legs, so her feet lined up with mine. Even though she was barely an inch shorter than me, she had to spread her legs wider. I must have a longer inseam than she did. She reached out, and I took her hands. They were soft, but she had a firm grip. I leaned back, pulling her down into a stretch that was sure to lengthen those troublesome hamstrings. After an eight-count, she sat up and leaned back, pulling me into a deep stretch. Truth be told, I could have lay nearly flat on the mat without trouble, but I let her lead me. I suspected the same was true for her.

We repeated the stretch a couple of times then did our own post-run routines. When she stood up, I did too. I was trying to think of something appropriate to say, but she beat me to it.

"Listen, I've only been here for a few weeks, and I don't have any friends locally. I work from home, and my clients are all over the country, so it's just me. I don't know if you know what that's like—you probably have a million people to do stuff with."

I immediately pictured the only people I knew in town. They had recently cut me, rather decisively, out of their lives. "Actually, I'm in almost the exact same situation. I had someone—but that's over, and I'm flying solo too."

"Really? Well, I was wondering—would you like to hit the coffee place on the corner? I normally wouldn't go there looking all sweaty and gross, but if we're *both* basking in the post-workout glow, I won't feel self-conscious."

She may have been sweating, but she was as far from gross as a person could get. "You know what? I would love that."

Ten minutes later, we found ourselves sitting opposite each other at a four-top table. I had a latte, and Gemma had the same, but with vanilla.

"So, where did you move from?" I asked. "You seem really familiar, but I don't think we've ever met. At least, I'm pretty sure I would remember you."

She smiled. "I must have one of those familiar faces. I moved from California. I lived here for a while, but it didn't work out, so I went to the coast. I love the weather there, but the infrastructure is falling apart. I had to get out. Well that, and my money goes way farther here than out West! The cost of living was crazy, and I just couldn't justify it anymore."

"When did you live here?"

"It was like, nine or ten years ago."

"Wow! That's about when I was here. I went to school here, and I did the same thing. Things got... messy for me, so right around ten years ago, I transferred to a different school for my last couple of years, out in San Diego. I bounced around a bit, got my consultancy set up, and once it was stable and I had a good set of clients, I moved back here."

Gemma took a sip of her vanilla latte while she studied me. "What do you do?"

"I'm a technical writer. I take the instructions and stuff that engineers, and product designers put together, and then I translate it all to English that normal people can understand. It's pretty boring, but I enjoy it. You?"

"Finance analyst. I work from home, and I do a lot in spreadsheets. It's boring as hell—I bet more so than what you do—but I can set my own schedule most of the time. As long as my work gets done—and it's accurate—they don't care when or where I do it."

"Me too! The work is really droll, but I love the freedom it gives me. As long as I meet my deadlines, no one cares what I do."

A couple at a two-top in the corner caught Gemma's attention. She nodded their direction. "Check it out," she said.

I looked, without trying to seem like I was looking. The couple was a pair of young girls—maybe seventeen or eighteen—holding hands and sharing a scone over their coffees. The blonde with her back in the corner broke off part of the scone and fed it to the other girl, who bit playfully at her fingers, sucking on them for a second before releasing them to their owner. They laughed, and then the dark-haired girl leaned in and kissed the blonde.

"Good for them," Gemma said. "I like to see people happy and unafraid of being who they are."

I thought about that for a second. I had problems with that concept when I was younger, maybe a year or two older than those two girls. In fact, it was still an issue sometimes. I didn't exactly fit into a neat box. If Gemma knew me better, I'd think that was directed at me. "Yeah, it's not always easy to be that free."

She picked up on the tone of my voice. "Speaking from experience?"

"Yeah, sort of."

"Have you been with women before?"

The question startled me. I was still unsure of Gemma's motives. She said she was looking for a friend, but was she looking for more? And how would she know that I'd be receptive? She was really hot, and if she were a guy, I would be one hundred percent certain she was hitting on me. But women are... more complicated. I wasn't getting a good read on her, so I deflected. Maybe it was my recent troubles, but my radar was signaling me to be wary. "It's a really long story, and I'd prefer not to go into it. Not here. Not now."

Gemma could sense I was putting up a wall, so she changed the subject. "Can I see your phone?"

I eyed her suspiciously. "What for?"

"Just let me see it."

I reluctantly handed her my phone. She opened the text app, sent a message, and handed it back to me. I looked at what she wrote.

This is Gemma texting herself from your phone. Now you have her number.

"Why did you do that?" I asked.

Gemma registered the alarm on my face. "What? I just wanted to exchange numbers."

"Why did you do it that way? Who put you up to this?"

"Put me up to it? Darcy, no one did! I was just trying to be cute. I didn't think you'd get mad. I'm sorry, I didn't mean to upset you!"

I softened my posture but was still a little freaked out. "Look, I don't want you to think I'm crazy or anything, but I had an eerily similar exchange recently in my life, and things got out of control. It ended really badly. I'm still a little rattled by the whole thing."

"Part of that long story of yours?"

"Yeah, kind of. Call it part two. Part one was ten years ago, so this has been a long time in the making. Listen, thanks for the coffee, but I need to be going."

She seemed like she wasn't done questioning me, but she relented. Good thing, because I was done for the day. "Okay. It was good getting to know you a little bit, Darcy. I'll see you at the gym?"

I mumbled something like, "Yeah, see you around" and walked out. As I sat in my car, I watched her inside. She was finishing her latte alone, and I felt a little guilty. She said she was lonely and just wanted a friend, and I walked out on her. I had a hard time believing someone as gorgeous as she was lonely, but then again, I know I'm not ugly, and I was as alone as it gets. I'd wait to see what she did next before I passed judgment. We seemed quite similar to each other, and I didn't mind the view.

I backed out of my parking space and drove off before she saw me staring at her and decided that I was, indeed, a creep.

The Invitation

I skipped the gym the next day, choosing instead to run outdoors early, before work. It actually felt good. It was cool for a summer morning, so I was able to go out with a short-sleeved running shirt instead of a tank-top, and a pair of mid-length running shorts.

While I was running, I kept thinking over the coffee shop incident. I knew I'd overreacted, but the tactic Gemma used to trade numbers was just too familiar and brought up too many conflicting emotions. I should have controlled my emotions better, but I've never had a poker face.

And then her question about being with other women! She wasn't incorrect in her assumption, but it was presumptuous of her to assume. Who asks that question when they've just met a person—especially when they have no clue if the person swings that way?

Someone who can see you practically drooling over them. That's who, I thought. Thanks, Brain. When I want your input, I'll ask for it.

But she said she was just looking for a friend. And sometimes, people do say what they actually mean. And why was I acting like a teenager about this whole thing?

Because you ARE into her.

I told my brain to shut up and finished my run. I decided that I would go to the gym the next day, and if Gemma were there, I'd ask her out for a drink.

The next day I went to the gym at my regular time and scanned the massive room for Gemma but couldn't find her. I was surprised at the feeling of disappointment. Maybe my brain was right, and I DID like her after all.

I started out lifting weights. It was chest and back day, but I kept looking for Gemma. After fifteen minutes, I lost interest in the workout, and I went home.

That night, I dreamed about her. It wasn't a sexual dream, which I am prone to have, but just the two of us doing mundane things. I woke up, not remembering any details, but I felt happy. That was a welcome change.

The next day, I went back. I was mad at myself for not completing the workout yesterday. The one thing that has been constant in my life since my troubles in college has been working out. I'm almost thirty years old, and I refuse to let my body spread out and sag like I see happening to so many women my age. After aborting yesterday's session, I was going to work extra hard today.

And drag it out in case Gemma is late.

I told my brain to shut up again and got to work. I did a thirty-minute circuit, hitting the weights, focusing on back and chest, and I threw in some leg work for good measure. Squats are my butt's best friend, and my C-cups weren't going to stay firm on their own! When I was done, there was still no Gemma.

I put thirty minutes in on the treadmill, attempting to run at seven-point-five miles per hour like Gemma had. I made it ten minutes before I had to slow way down. I ended up walking the last few minutes. Still no Gemma. I supposed I'd have to wait to see her until tomorrow. I thought about texting her but told myself to wait. If I didn't see or hear from her tomorrow, then I'd reach out.

I skipped the stretch routine and went straight to the locker room. I'd worked extra hard and was too sweaty to leave without a shower. I stripped out of my shorts and top, wrapped up in a towel, and grabbed my shower kit. I slipped my feet into a pair of flip-flops and headed to the shower stalls.

After pulling the outer curtain shut, I hung my towel on the hook and turned the water on, setting it to a warm—not hot—temperature and stepped in. I thought again about Gemma asking me if I'd been with a woman. A super-hot, very fit woman asked me that. She had to want me, right? She'd been forcing me to stare at that ass of hers while running. She *must* have ulterior motives.

Of course, even if she did, how bad was that? It's not like I hadn't thought about her in that way. After all, I'd been staring at that perfect ass while running in place, and I let my mind wander. I'd seen the muscles in her thighs when she'd done squats and imagined what those legs would feel like wrapped around my head. I may have been dumped in the worst possible way recently, but I wasn't completely dead from the waist down.

I moaned and realized my hand had drifted down to my pussy. I was absentmindedly teasing my clitoris, thinking about Gemma! I pulled my hand away. I couldn't do that here. I mean, I *could*—I'd masturbated in riskier places before—but I was worried I wouldn't be able to keep quiet, and after the events of the last few weeks, I wanted to keep a low profile. I soaped up, washed my hair, rinsed it out twice, and turned the shower off.

As I walked back to my locker, I could feel that my lips and clit were swollen, and that made me even hornier. I began to think about what I was going to do to myself when I got home.

And there was Gemma. She was wearing Lycra running shorts and a coral tank top with a low-cut front. The supportive bustline was linked by a swatch of black elastic, and I knew it had an open back with corset laces. I'd seen her in this top last week. It looked fabulous on her. Of course, everything did.

I smiled as I approached her, trying to act nonchalant. *Yeah, play it cool. Hi Gemma, I was not just touching myself in the shower, thinking about you!* I told my brain to shut up. "Hi, Gemma! It's good to see you. I—uh—I missed you yesterday. Er, and today."

Smooth.

She grinned back. "Sorry. I had a bunch of meetings. I do enjoy a lot of freedom, but every now and then I have to adhere to someone else's schedule."

"Well, it's not like we had a date. Er, plans, I mean."

Nailed it.

"Speaking of plans, what are you doing tonight?"

My heart jumped. "Tonight?" *Nothing. You're doing nothing. Tell her.* I cleared my throat. "I don't have any plans." Sometimes I *do* listen to my brain.

"Well, I just had to pay some unexpected bills, so cash is kinda tight. I know it's late notice—I should have texted, but time got away from me—but I was going to see if you wanted to get something to eat. However, given my cash flow situation, I was wondering if you'd like to come over to my place instead of going out. I have some chicken that needs to be cooked today or thrown out. I hate wasting food, so you'd be doing me a favor."

I thought about it for about a half-second before I said, "Yeah, that sounds great. What can I bring?"

"How about a loaf of French bread?"

We both laughed. As if that many carbs were going to pass either of our lips. "Why don't I bring some wine?"

"That would be wonderful. I'm cooking Caprese, so make it a red." She stood up, and I noticed she looked me up and down in my towel as she did so. "I have some more errands to run. See you at six? I'll text you my address."

"Six sounds great."

She left, and I hurriedly got dressed and left without drying my hair or applying any makeup. I needed to get home and get ready.

Dinner

I fretted over what to wear. I wanted to look nice—Gemma had never seen me in anything other than workout clothes—but I also didn't want to overdo it. Nothing too sexy—I didn't want her to think I was trying to seduce her. I needed to proceed carefully because there was the possibility that she only wanted to be friends. I was reasonably sure she wanted more, but I didn't want to tip my hand yet, not after what I'd been through with the last relationship crashing and burning. I didn't need to kill this one before it got off the ground.

I went with what I call suburban casual. I wore a pair of stretchy jeans and a white spaghetti-strap top with crisscrossed strings between the straps in front that helped camouflage my cleavage. I tried it without a bra, but my nipples were poking out, and I didn't want to send the wrong message. I shrugged out of the top, put on a low cut, strapless bra, and slipped into the top again. Much better.

I followed Waze to a lovely two-bedroom house. I think realtors would call it "cozy." It was in the older part of town, and like my place, the garage was a detached, single-car affair behind the home. Following her directions, I pulled all the way to the back and parked off to the side of the driveway. As I walked to the back door, I could smell the food and realized I was hungry.

She answered the door in the same coral top as before. To be fair, if it looked as good on me as it did on her, I would never take it off. While it was a workout top, the corset straps made it suitable for casual wear too. She had swapped the tight Lycra for a looser pair of olive-colored shorts with an integrated fabric belt tied into a bow in the front. My suburban casual was the right call.

I stepped inside, and the smell of the chicken cooking on the stove was a thousand times more potent than it was outside. My salivary glands cramped; it smelled so good. "Oh my god, what is that?"

"Caprese chicken. Maybe it's my Italian heritage, but the balsamic vinegar cooking drives me crazy. Trust me, you're going to love it."

"I didn't know you were cooking so fancy."

"It's effortless, actually. Takes about twenty minutes to fix and uses like five ingredients. It's no trouble at all. You're doing me a favor because I hate leftovers, and I had too much chicken for one person to eat." She handed me a corkscrew. "You want to open that wine?"

"Of course! Can I help you with dinner?"

"No help needed. It's almost done."

I handed her a glass of wine, and she sipped it. "Oh, that's good. Solid choice. Make yourself at home. You can do a self-guided tour if you want while I finish up."

"You don't mind me poking around?"

"Of course not. Oh, if you need the restroom, use the one in my bedroom. There's something wrong with the one in the hallway, and I haven't had the money to get someone to work on it."

"I can take a look at it. I had to fix mine a while back. Went to Home Depot and everything. I'm a pro." The mention of Home Depot brought back a series of memories that ended badly. I pushed them into the back of my mind.

Gemma laughed. "I might take you up on that, but another time. Not tonight."

I walked through her house. The kitchen and dining nook took up the rear corner closest to the garage. Outside the kitchen, a hallway led to two bedrooms. The one on the front of the house was small and was clearly her office. She had a loveseat against one wall and a desk and laptop connected to two large monitors on the other. I noticed there was no closet in the room, which seemed odd.

I walked across the hall to Gemma's bedroom, which was much bigger than her office. She had a spacious king-sized bed, which was made up, of course. A six-drawer dresser occupied the wall opposite the bed. The walk-in closet had a wide pocket door that was half-open. I peeked inside and saw an assortment of tops and dresses, summer colors only, and a long rack that ran the width of the floor with three rows of shoes, from athletic to what I liked to call "fuck me" pumps. Even though she told me to take a tour, I didn't want to get caught snooping.

I went to her bathroom and was immediately jealous. What the house lacked in living space, it made up for with this bathroom. A two-piece counter with a makeup station took up most of the outside wall. I noticed that Gemma used many of the same brands of makeup that I did. Of course, Gemma didn't wear a lot of makeup, as she was blessed with a beautiful complexion and dark Italian skin that didn't need much help. She wore her eyes on the smoky side, but that was about the extent of it. I, in contrast, had a light Irish complexion and counted myself fortunate to have smooth, clear skin.

But that shower! That was what impressed me the most. It had no door or curtain, just a short, knee-high wall with an opening on one end for the entry. It was six feet deep and ran the width of the room. It had a built-in bench on the far end that wrapped around the length of the back wall. On the ceiling, there were multiple rainfall showerheads, and on the wall, at the end above the bench, there was a detachable handheld showerhead with multiple stream and pressure settings. I recognized it immediately because I had a similar one. It was also the result of a Home Depot project. I wondered if Gemma used hers in the same way I used mine on occasion.

I rejoined Gemma in the kitchen, where she was plating the chicken breasts with a side of cauliflower and a small patch of Caesar salad.

"Just in time! It's ready!" Gemma beamed.

"Gemma, I could live in that shower. Oh, my god! It's amazing!"

"Right? That was done by the previous owner. They took out the closet in the second bedroom to expand the master so they could do that bath. To be honest, that's why I bought this place."

"That's a good reason! I'm surprised you even shower at the gym!"

"Well, I like being naked in public, so that fulfills my kink."

I was stunned for a moment before Gemma said, "Kidding! Sort of. It all depends on my schedule. Sometimes I do just come home to shower, but only if I'm not too sweaty and gross."

"You never look gross."

"Aw! You're sweet. Come on, let's eat."

Too Much Wine

After dinner, Gemma put a downtempo chillout station on Pandora, and we moved from the kitchen to the family room. We sat on the couch—me, on the right side, and her on the left. I noticed that we simply took our spots, like a couple who already knew each other's preferences.

The Caprese chicken was amazing, and before we sat down, I made Gemma send me a link to the recipe. If it were as easy as she said it was, I would be cooking that dish a few times a month.

She poured me another glass of wine, my third. I smiled and took a sip. "Are you trying to get me drunk?"

"No! It's just a habit when I see an empty glass. I used to tend bar in college."

"That's funny! I used to go to a lot of bars in college!"

She laughed her musical laugh. I loved hearing it.

"What else did you do in college? What was the craziest thing you did?"

I scowled. "We're back to this again, are we?"

"Don't run out on me again! You just made it sound so mysterious, I've been dying to know what happened. Based on your reaction in the coffee shop,

I think it involves a woman, but that can't be all there is to it. I mean, you can't get coffee these days without seeing girls making out. Hell, *I've* been with a woman before."

I'd be lying if I didn't feel a tingle when she said that, but I wasn't sure she wanted to go where this conversation would take us.

She persisted. "So, if it's not a woman, it must be worse than that. Threesome?"

I didn't say anything.

"*Four*some?"

I just kept staring.

"Donkey show? *Please* tell me it's a donkey show!"

I couldn't keep a straight face after that one. "How the hell do you go from foursome to donkey show? You skipped right over orgy."

A sly smile spread across her face. "An honest-to-god orgy? Like with Hef in the grotto? You *must* tell me all about it now! Spare no detail."

I sighed. "You're going to think I'm a tramp. I don't want to kill our friendship before it even starts."

"I promise you, even if you went raw dog on an entire frat house, I wouldn't think you're a tramp. I've done some crazy things too, and besides, you're grown up now. It's all a part of who you are."

I tried to deflect the conversation. "Well, let's hear your stories first then!"

She shook her head, her raven-black hair shimmering around her head. "No. My house, my rules. You go first."

I sighed again. I was afraid if I told Gemma the story, she'd be disgusted with me and send me home. But on the other hand, if we were going to be friends, or whatever was going on here, she needed to know me and accept me for who I am. There's no way I could keep it secret now that it was half in the open. "Well, it's funny you should mention a frat house..."

"Shut *up!*" She topped off her wine and offered me the bottle, which I gladly took. "You did *not!* Tell me *everything!*"

I emptied the bottle into my glass. Gemma was looking at me with bright, expectant eyes. I felt like I was at camp, sitting in the bunkhouse with flashlights talking about what guy we thought was cute. Except this camp had just two people, and we were not going be as innocent as that. I took a long pull of the wine, feeling its warmth spread through me. Maybe it was the alcohol taking over, but I was about to share something with a woman I barely knew that I hadn't shared with anyone in a decade.

I let out a long breath. "You really want to hear this?"

She was eager. "Yes. More than anything at this moment."

"Okay, here goes, but remember, you asked for it. It was ten years ago, and I was in my sophomore year of college, or what I called my second freshman year..."

Forgetting Phillip
Ten Years Ago

It was a Friday night, and the Sigma Omega guys were having a party. My roommates, Sheila and Kelly, were dying to go. They were alright as far as roommates go, but they insisted on dragging me out all the time when I didn't want to go anywhere, and this was one of those nights. I was determined to sulk because I'd just broken up with my boyfriend. His name was Phillip—not Phil, Phillip—and he was a year older than me, and he was good looking, but he was a dick. He dumped me for a girl who went down on him in the bathroom at Hennigan's Bar. Classy, I know.

"Come on," Kelly pleaded. "Phillip is a dick. Don't you dare sit here tonight and pine for him. You know he's not alone tonight. You need to go out with us and find a rebound guy and get that loser out of your mind."

"Yeah," Sheila piled on. "Here, have some liquid courage and get lubed up."

Of the two, I liked Sheila more than Kelly. She was kind, and honest, and would do things for you— you know, like a real friend. Kelly only did things if it served her interest or she got something in return. Fair-weathered friend, I believe, was the term. If she were going to the mall, she'd give you a ride, but if it was five minutes out of her way, forget it. But she had parents who ensured she was never late with the rent, so I put up with her sometimes shitty attitude.

Sheila handed me a double shot glass filled with tequila. In my experience, very few nights had ever gone well when they started out with tequila. I took the shot and tipped it back, then fought the urge to cough it back up.

"Yeah! Atta girl!" Sheila praised me and handed a glass to Kelly, who downed it and gagged worse than I did. I hoped for a second that she'd throw up, and we'd stay home. Alas, she recovered her composure.

"Is that what you're wearing?" Kelly asked me once she'd recovered from the shot and could speak.

I looked down at my sweater and capris. "Yes?" It definitely came out as more of a question than a statement.

"No, not to a Sig Om party. Come on."

She dragged me to my room and picked out a halter top and a knee-length, flowy denim skirt. I stripped down and dressed in the outfit she picked out for me. I was a B-cup back then, so I didn't bother with a bra. I walked out to the living room and did a dramatic twirl. "Satisfied?"

Kelly nodded. "Much better."

We walked the half mile to the party. Uber hadn't made its way to town yet, and we were too cheap to pay for a cab. Plus, we knew we were probably going to get pretty wasted and didn't want to be tempted to drive. Kelly was really keen to go to this party because some guy from one of her classes was in the frat and invited her. Of course, he told her to bring some friends, so that meant Sheila and I *had* to go.

The ratio of women-to-men at the party was easily five-to-one. The frat guys really liked to stack the odds in their favor. Of course, we got in for free and had drinks pushed on us right away. I was tipsy in no time, but it wasn't really my scene. I'd made an appearance, and that fulfilled Kelly's obligation to whatever guy she was trying to hook up with, but I wasn't really having fun.

I pulled Kelly close to me. "I think I'm going to head back," I said to her. "I'm just not into this scene tonight."

"Don't go!" she pleaded with me. "You need to get back out there so you can move on from Phillip. I can't take any more of your moping around about him." She even found a way to make my breakup about her. "Rebound guy, remember? This house is full of them. Plus, I'm looking for Todd, the guy from my chem lab. Just stick around for a few more minutes, okay?"

I reluctantly agreed. Sheila brought me a drink—some sort of mixed concoction that smelled like prune juice and tasted like Dr. Pepper. She handed it to me and gave Kelly a wink. I sipped it, and it was good. Too good. It was gone before I knew it, and within a couple minutes, my head was really swimming.

That's when I saw him. Tall, dark, all that. He came over to me and hit me up with a few clichés—"I haven't seen you here before, where have you been hiding?" and "What do you do for fun, besides being hot?"—dumb stuff like that. Usually, I'd laugh at that sort of come-on—I mean, does that work on anyone? But, I was well on my way to drunk, and the edges around my vision were getting fuzzy.

He finally just came straight at me. "So, what would happen if I kissed you?"

I blinked at the question. Had this guy never kissed anyone before? Did he really not know what would happen? These were the kind of questions that were going through my head, so that should have been a red flag that something was amiss. But, I also heard Kelly's voice in my head saying, "Rebound guy." So, I finally just said, "Only one way to find out."

I remember his lips were rough, chapped. They felt scratchy on my face and neck as he nuzzled and kissed me. He ran his hands over the outside of my halter top, and I felt my nipples respond. His hands wandered, stroking my thighs, lifting my skirt, I'm sure flashing my underwear at others in the room. I was wearing white panties with a red heart on them. I'd just recently got them—part of a set with different emojis on them—so I didn't mind if people saw them. Wherever his hands touched me, I felt them for a few seconds, like a replay of the touch. It was a wild feeling, and I wanted more. I knew I should stop him, but everything felt so good I just let him run his hands all over me. He snuck a hand inside my halter top and found my breasts and my hard nipples. I gasped when he tweaked them. *Fuck, that feels good! More of that!* I did not tell my brain to shut up. Aloud, I just moaned.

That's when Kelly came over and grabbed my arm and pulled me away from him. "Darcy, what the fuck do you think you're doing?"

I was confused. "Rebound guy, remember? I gonna let him put it in me." I was finding it difficult to talk.

She was angry, but I had no idea why. "Seriously? A house full of men and you had to go for him? Of all the people, you had to pick the one guy I wanted? Some friend you are."

Ah, so that was it. This was Todd. "How I supposed to know? You two poured liquor in me and tol' me to get laid, and that's what I'm doing. He never even introduced hisself."

Her lips were pursed so tight if you put a piece of coal between them, she'd spit out a diamond. "I think you were right before. It's time for you to go home."

There was no way I was leaving. I wanted more touching and petting from Mr. Magic Hands. "No way, Kel. My puss is on *fire* right now, and he's got the equipment to put it out." Honestly, I had no idea why I was talking like that—it wasn't normal for me, but it was how I felt at that moment.

Sheila came over and saw Kelly's angry face. "What's going on, guys? Why are you pissed off?"

"Little Miss 'I don't wanna go out tonight' had my guy's hands all over her, flashing her stupid heart panties to the room."

Sheila, the good friend, took my side. "You've barely talked to him, Kel."

"I have too! He invited me here tonight!"

"He invited you and as many friends as you could bring. This was hardly a date." She jerked a thumb in my direction. "And if you haven't noticed, the ecstasy is kicking in."

I looked at Sheila. "Wait, what? Ecstasy? What?"

She laughed. "Don't be mad, but I dosed your last drink. You really needed to loosen up and enjoy yourself. You'll be fine. It was Kelly's idea, but I thought it was a good one. I really wanted you to have fun tonight."

I should have been furious that my friend and roommate had drugged me, but I was feeling too good to get mad. "Can't take it back now, can we?"

Kelly folded her arms across her chest. "No, but you could leave."

Yeah, I was high on ecstasy in a house full of guys who would probably love to bang me, and everything that touched me felt incredible. "I'm not going anywhere. I have rebounding to do."

"Look, Darcy, either you leave, or I'm leaving. You're being a total bitch about this."

"You told me to get laid, and Sheila gave me the sexy drug. I'm not going home when I feel this good."

"Fine," she said and turned on her heel.

"She'll get over it," Sheila said. "Go get some cock. I'll cool her down." She winked at me and took off after Kelly.

I turned back to Todd, who had been standing a few feet away. "Where were we?" I asked.

"Well, we were making out pretty hard, but that chick from my chem class tried to cock block you."

"I don't have a cock."

"Would you like one?"

I walked into that one. I could have said no. I *should* have said no. But two things were going on in my head. One, I was high and horny on X. And two, I was pissed at Kelly. If Todd wanted me instead of her, he could have me. But I had to play *a little* hard to get.

"My roommate is mad cause you touched my boob and flashed my panties at the room. I don't want to cause trouble between you two."

"Who? Kelly? I don't like her. She's hung up on me or something, but she's not my type. Not like you. You're like, super hot. Are you down to have some fun?"

"Well, I *am* at a frat party, so that's pretty much a yes."

"Like, wild fun. The kind that they make movies about?"

I squinted at him. "I'm not making a porno with you, if that's what you're hinting at."

"No, no, no, nothing like that. Just... maybe some more people involved."

My impulse this time was to say no, but I had a flash of me coming back to the apartment with my tail between my legs, five minutes after Kelly and Sheila left. I didn't want to give Kelly the satisfaction. "I'm listening."

I swear Todd did that *Yes!* fist pump in his head so hard I could see it. "Alright, come with me."

He took my hand, and I let him lead me to the basement steps. Red flag, right? Has anything good ever happened in a basement when you started the night doing tequila shots, and your roommates dosed you with X? I didn't think so. Still, Kelly was such a shrill harpy, I felt it was my duty to have sex with this man. Or men. Whatever.

He led me down the stairs to a large room with about fifteen guys scattered around. Whoa, I wasn't ready to do fifteen guys. I spotted a woman sitting in an oversized leather chair, but she was the only other female in the room.

Todd looked over at one of the other guys and called out, "Hey Boomer, is she good to go?"

Boomer returned a thumbs up. "GTG, man. GTG."

I looked around, and the place was, to quote *Van Wilder*, decorated in early fuck. A large, cushion-armed leather sectional sofa dominated the room, with the other woman sitting in the oversized matching chair next to it. There were a few lamps scattered around with red bulbs in them. Music was playing from speakers that I couldn't see. I remember hearing *Too Drunk To Fuck* by Buckcherry, and I wondered how many of these guys it applied to.

Todd led me to the woman in the big leather chair. I don't remember much about her, other than she was stunningly pretty. Short, black hair, long tan legs. Todd nudged me. "Go sit by her," he said.

I was going to ask why, but he gave me another push. The woman patted the cushion next to her, so I walked over and sat down. I don't know what her perfume was, but I got one sniff of it, and I felt my face get flush. I got a tingle down below, and I felt what I call the "quickening" surge through me. It must have been pure pheromones, or the ecstasy was affecting my sense of smell, too. I felt my nipples harden again and remember thinking I should have worn a bra. "Holy shit, you smell nice," I blurted out. I know, smooth.

She reached over and stroked my face, her fingers leaving tingles down my cheek. "Thank you! Do you know why they brought you down here?"

I shook my head.

"They want to watch us fuck each other."

I was stunned but also spellbound by her. My face still tingled where she'd touched me, and I know this sounds cliché, but I felt myself get wet.

"Have you ever been with a girl?"

I gulped. I had never even considered it. "No."

"Would you like to?"

The alternative would be running for the door, going home, and admitting to Kelly that I was in over my head. Of course, if I'd let her have Todd, she'd be in that chair. Would she do it? Fuck a girl in front of a dozen guys? And what were they going to get out of it? So many unanswered questions.

This is one of those "change you forever" moments. Seriously, brain? That wasn't helpful. "I don't know," I finally said. "What—um—what do I have to do?"

She traced a line down my chest, circling the bumps where my nipples stuck out, leaving an electrified trail wherever she touched. She dragged her finger down my stomach and put it inside the waistband of my skirt, running it back and forth. My stomach twitched in response like it was a separate entity from me.

She leaned in, so close her lips were brushing my ear. Unlike Todd's, her lips were as smooth as glass, and soft, and warm, and sent shivers down to my pussy and back up. "Why don't I show you first, and then you can do it to me?"

This woman, whose name I never got, licked the outer edge of my ear, taking my earlobe into her mouth and gently biting it. Her hands were still running around my body, one of them under my halter, her nails scratching at my stomach, and the other on the outside of my thigh, under my skirt, tracing the hem of my panties. Everything felt amazing and perfect and *right*. I let out an involuntary moan.

"Well," she said, "Is that a yes?"

"Uh-huh," I heard myself reply. I relaxed and gave myself over to her.

More Wine!

I paused in my storytelling, trying to gauge where Gemma's head was at, but her expression didn't give me anything. *I bet she's excellent at poker,* I thought. I drank more wine to stall for time, draining the remainder of my glass.

"Don't stop now!" she finally exclaimed.

"So, this isn't too much information, too soon?"

"Oh, no! I'm riveted over here! This is better than any night out. You're making me flush! I'm delighted you agreed to come over tonight."

"Well, I guess I am too. I'm gonna need more wine to get through the next part."

"Say no more!" She swung her legs off the couch, and for a split second, I caught a glimpse of her panties up the leg of her shorts.

I was only slightly surprised to feel a thrill run through me at the image. I don't know if it was the wine or reliving the story, but I was feeling pretty flush myself.

Gemma returned with a new bottle of wine. It was the same brand I brought over to pair with the balsamic vinegar used in the chicken recipe. She saw me looking at it. "I know, right? We think alike, apparently."

She filled my glass, and I took a long sip. I'd be taking an Uber home tonight, for sure.

Gemma sat back on the couch, tucking her legs under her, bouncing on the cushion. She shook her head, and that long, black hair flipped around. It was spellbinding.

"Okay, intermission's over. Get on with this story!"

"Alright, but it gets pretty bad."

"I want to hear it. All of it."

I took another sip and resumed the story where I'd left off.

All the Way, and Then Some
Ten Years Ago

So, we were in this big leather chair, and this woman whose name I didn't get, was whispering in my ear. I felt warm in all the right places, and I'd just agreed to let her have her way with me, with a small crowd watching.

She kissed me, full on the mouth, her tongue darting in and out like a hummingbird. Her soft lips pressed into mine, and she did that thing where she bit my lower lip and pulled it out a little. I love that! At that point, I was all in. I started kissing her back, running my hands up and down her back, squeezing her ass.

She ran her hand over my breasts, grabbing them this time instead of just grazing the nipples. I arched my back to make them more available to her. I didn't even feel her untie the strap around my neck, but she must have, because she pulled my halter top down and put her mouth on first one nipple, then the other.

I moaned not just because it felt good—and it may have been the ecstasy, but it *really* felt good—but it clicked in my head that it was a *girl* with my nipple in her mouth. This was taboo! I felt the quickening. Electricity surged through me, and I moaned with pleasure.

The sound jolted me out of my reverie for a moment, and I saw that all around the room, men—boys, really—had their cocks out, stroking them. I was alarmed and was about to say something like, "What the fuck are you doing?" when the woman lifted my left leg into the air. My skirt rode up, and she started kissing my calf, working her way toward my knee. The masturbating frat boys were forgotten for a moment.

She held my leg with her right hand, and her left stroked my other thigh, working higher until she found my pubic mound. She rubbed it outside my panties while she kissed her way north on my left leg, past my knee now.

I closed my eyes and rolled my head back. I'm sure the ecstasy helped, but her hand pressing and rubbing on me was sending wave after wave of pleasure cascading out from my pussy through the rest of my body, and back again.

Her mouth was mid-thigh now, and I was quivering, eagerly anticipating what would come next. She slid my panties to one side and kissed that sensitive spot where the thigh meets the body, and I almost came. I knew she was going to lick my pussy next. A woman was going to put her mouth on me. It was naughty and exciting, and it felt *good*.

Except I was wrong. What happened next was one of the frat boys, um, made a delivery on my chest. I was shocked and on the verge of anger. The other guys laughed at him and shoved him out of the way.

"And the first contestant drops out!" Boomer shouted.

"Fuck this" was on the verge of leaving my mouth when the woman's tongue parted my lips and traced a path to my clitoris. The scandal of a woman putting her mouth on my pussy made me forget about the boys again. It made me forget about everything other than her, and what she was doing to me.

I was so wet that she easily slid her fingers inside me. Two? Three? I don't know. But between the rhythmic pulsing of her finger and her tongue doing calligraphy on me, I was lost in her actions. My whole existence was narrowed down to my pussy and her tongue. I vaguely heard more cheers go up from the crowd, but I didn't pay attention to them. I was breathing hard, moaning, my hips rising an inch or two every time she moved her hand.

Now, it's not like I hadn't been eaten out before, but this was a whole different thing. My orgasm was building. I heard another cheer, only now it seemed like they were cheering for me. I was climbing up a monstrous wave of pleasure. My hips were bucking against her mouth, and she pressed back like she'd been eating pussy her entire life. I was moaning and grinding against her mouth. I grabbed her hair and pulled her face down tighter against me. Another cheer went up. I never wanted this to end. Every nerve ending was exploding. I was no longer in my body but watching from above. When I came, I swear I levitated out of that chair. My pussy pulsed so hard I think my Kegels pushed her fingers out, and for the first time in my life, I squirted.

I collapsed into the leather chair, my chest, arms, and hair sticky with cum from whatever weird bukkake beat-off game the boys were playing. I was out of breath, and my pussy was vibrating in the afterglow.

The crowd fell silent for a moment. I guess the boys were waiting to see what I was going to do. I released the woman's hair, and she looked up at me, her face dripping with my cum, a smile spread across her visage.

She climbed up my body, feline in her motions. She pressed herself against me, not seeming to care that I was sticky from the boy's spent fluids. She bit my ear again and purred, "My turn."

I stood on wobbly legs and let her take the chair. She took her shirt off, exposing her B-cups. I hadn't noticed she wasn't wearing a bra, but that might be because she had the firmest tits I'd ever seen. I removed my halter top all the way, then unfastened the button on my skirt and let it drop. My white, heart emblazoned panties were soaked, so I slid them off.

"Holy shit," someone said.

The woman took the cue and slipped her shorts and G-string off. I straddled her and leaned in close, our bare breasts touching, the sensation of her nipples brushing over mine sending fits through my pussy. It was my turn to bite her ear. I pulled on her lobe, sucking on it for a moment before whispering, "I've never eaten pussy before. You need to tell me if I can do something better."

I sat up, and she squeezed my breasts while I teased her nipples into hard buds. "You know what you like. Just do that," she purred. I started kissing and licking her neck and chest, and she pushed my head down toward her pussy. "Just go for it," she instructed me. "I'm ready for you." I slid off her and found myself on my knees, face to face with my first-ever vagina. She was waxed completely bald, where my pubic hair was the classic pie-shaped bush, carefully trimmed, but not waxed. I found it to be beautiful, and I decided at that moment that the first chance I got, I was getting waxed clean.

If you'd told me that morning that by the end of the day, I'd be having lesbian sex with someone I didn't know, in front of a crowd of ejaculating frat boys, I'd have said: "There's no fucking way that's ever happening." But here I was, about to eat a stranger's pussy. I trembled in anticipation. Did I have the nerve to go through with it?

I kissed it, and I felt her tremble. I licked it once, apprehensive about what it would taste like. To my surprise, it didn't have much flavor, but if I had to describe it, I would say it tasted like electricity. She *smelled* like sex, and it was intoxicating. She was already wet, so when I put a finger inside her, it slipped in easy.

"More," she moaned.

I slid a second and then a third finger into her while licking her like an ice cream cone.

"Not so hard," she whispered. "Go from top to bottom using the underside of your tongue. That's the pressure you should use."

I took her direction, using the bottom of my tongue to lick her. I used that as a gauge and reverted to using the top with less force. Based on her response, I had it dialed in.

"Now, draw a picture," she said. "A flower, or a forest."

I began tracing a daisy on her pussy lips and clit, imagining her trying to figure out what I was making. She responded by pulling my hair. "Holy shit, girl, you eat pussy like a pro!"

I felt something poke me from behind. I clenched up and looked over my shoulder. Todd was there, touching my vagina. I had a fleeting thought of *in for a penny, in for a pound,* and before I knew I'd even thought the words, my mouth said, "Fuck me," and I dropped my back a little and spread my legs, making myself as available to him as I could.

I turned my attention back to the woman, reaching up with a free hand to stroke and pinch her nipples, flicking my tongue on her, sliding my fingers in and out.

Todd entered me, just a little at first, then more, then on the third stroke, he went balls deep, as they say. He pumped against me and drove my face into the woman's pussy, making her cry out. I could feel his balls hitting me, slapping into my clit. I clenched on him and heard him say, "Oh my god!"

The woman was bucking against me, screaming, and I felt Todd release everything inside me, his cock pulsing several times. He pulled out, leaving me empty, and I could feel his cum running down the inside of my thighs.

The woman cried out, "Fuck her!" Within seconds, another cock was sliding into me. I glanced back and saw Boomer thrusting his hips like a rabbit. The pinball action, his cock slamming into me, my face slamming into the woman's pussy, was a perverse rhythm. Boomer came even faster than Todd. "Next!" I shouted, hungry for more. I'm sure it was the effects of the ecstasy, but I felt so powerful at that moment. Men were practically diving over each other to fuck me, one after another, not even caring that I was a mess of other men's cum. I had my face buried in this woman's pussy, and she was screaming in pleasure. When she came, I came, and the last guy came inside me. The three of us, all cumming at once, all crying out, was fucking amazing. Her cum shot out of her, not a squirt like mine was, but forcefully enough that it ran over my fingers and up my nose. Her smell was like a savory perfume.

I climbed up into the chair, and she wrapped her arms around me. "Are you okay?" she asked.

"Mmm. I feel like a whore. A dirty, satisfied, cum drenched whore. I fucking loved this."

She stroked my hair, and when another boy came over, cock in hand, trying to line it up with my pussy, she pulled me tight to her and said, "No. We're done. Fuck off."

He started to protest, and another frat boy, one I hadn't seen before, walked over. "Beat it, Fudge Stripe," he said. He had two blankets under his arm. "Ladies, would you like to shower?"

"What time is it?" I asked.

"Quarter after one."

Holy shit! I thought. We'd gone downstairs around eleven! How could it have been more than *two hours* of sucking and fucking? It had to be the drug, compressing time in addition to making me insanely horny.

"Yes," the woman said, "a shower would be nice." She started to move, so I stood up. I literally felt like I was head-to-toe covered in cum. I guess that's because I was.

The man offered us each a blanket. While we covered up in them, I looked around. "Where the fuck are my clothes?"

He wrapped one of the blankets around me. "I took them. All your stuff is locked in my room, your clothes are in the wash. I figured you'd want to go home as clean as when you came here."

"Oh, well... that's nice," I said. "So, which number were you?"

He looked confused.

"When did you fuck me?"

"I didn't. I was there to ensure things didn't get out of hand."

I raised my eyebrows at him.

"What I mean is, if either of you said enough was enough, I would ensure that everything stopped as soon as you said so. Like I just did."

"Oh," I said.

"How often do you guys do this?" the woman asked him.

"As often as we get a couple of willing women. The guys put money in the pot and bet on who lasts the longest beating off. The ones jerking it are the first years. Second years and up, we allow to..."

"Fuck us," I finished his sentence for him.

"Yeah."

"Why didn't you join in?"

"I just don't feel right about it. I mean, I know that sounds dumb since I help facilitate, but I'd rather be with someone in a more... intimate setting. And someone has to be the zookeeper for the rest of those apes."

We'd climbed out of the basement, ascended two more flights of stairs, and walked halfway down a long hallway.

"Here we are," he said, pushing a door open. "Cleanest shower in the house. I put out towels, there's soap, and shampoo in there." He pointed to a chair a few feet away. "I'll be out here, making sure no one bothers you."

We climbed into the shower together and took our time soaping each other up. The woman took care to clean me down below, as well as she could. We took turns washing each other's hair, and we pressed our bodies together. I loved the feel of her hairless, soapy torso against mine, the way our breasts slid over each other. She kissed me tenderly, running her hands up and down my back. It was sweet.

The frat boy knocked on the door. "Everything okay in there?"

I peeked around the curtain and saw clock the read 2:00. Oops! "Yes," I said as the woman turned the water off. "We'll be right out."

We toweled off and stepped out of the shower. The woman wrapped the towel around her head, standing naked in front of me. She really was gorgeous, but I was focused more on her perfect body than anything else. I had just—what? Fucked her? I didn't know what to call it, but we had been as intimate as two lovers can be. I felt different than I had at the start of the night, and not just because I'd had my mouth on her gorgeous pussy.

"Well," she said. "Let's go take care of our white knight, shall we?"

Completion

Y ou can't leave me hanging," Gemma begged. "And you actually did all that? You're not making it up because I joked about raw-dogging an entire frat?"

I felt ashamed. "No, I'm not making it up. You can go find another friend now, I won't be offended."

She slid across the couch in one smooth motion. "Why would I want to do that? You may be the most interesting woman I've ever met. I want to know everything about you. Why would I want to find another friend?"

"I don't know. It just sounds bad when I tell the story. I was Slutty McSlutterson. And it didn't exactly pay dividends, as you'll find out soon enough."

"Darcy, you did that stuff because you wanted to, and there's nothing wrong with that. The ecstasy and liquor may have loosened your inhibitions a little..."

I rolled my eyes at her.

"Okay, a *lot*, but that fearless warrior is inside you. If a guy went and had sex with a bunch of girls like that, he'd never stop bragging about it. He'd be sixty years old and still beating off to it. Don't you ever be ashamed about having that kind of appetite.

Find another friend? Darcy, I'm in awe of you. But, I want to know how the night ended." She stroked my arm and held my hand, lacing her fingers into mine. "Please?"

I looked her in the eye. She was intense and sincere and disarming. Her expression made me want to please her.

"Okay," I relented.

The White Knight's Lair
Ten Years Ago

The woman opened the bathroom door and walked into the hall naked. I followed, wrapped in my towel.

The man stood up and stared at her body, then averted his gaze. "All clean?"

"Yep," we both said at the same time.

"Great! Well, your clothes aren't dry yet, so I guess we could..."

"Go to your room," the woman finished the sentence for him.

He paused, doing some mental gymnastics, based on his expression. "Okay," he finally said. We walked down the hall, and he opened a door for us. The room was clean, or at least clean for a frat house. There were two beds, one each on opposite sides of the room. "My roommate is gone for the weekend," he explained.

"His loss," the woman said. She rubbed his groin, and he initially pulled back.

"No, you don't have to..."

"This is happening... what's your name?" she asked.

"Peter."

"This is happening, Peter." She looked at me and nodded at the door. I closed it and locked it.

"Now," the woman started, unfastening his belt, "here's how this will go down. You've been watching all this crazy sex all night. You're probably primed and ready to pop. I'm going to take care of you, then you're going to take care of my friend. Understand?" She pulled his pants down, taking his boxers at the same time. His cock sprang up, already hard.

I gasped. It was ten inches long if it was an inch. It wasn't as thick as others I've seen or had inside me—that night, even—but *damn* was it a sight to behold.

The woman took him by the cock and led him over to the roommate's bed. She pushed him down, making him lie flat, leaving his tower of flesh sticking straight up in the air.

She wrapped a hand around his shaft and began stroking it. He moaned right away. She licked her other hand and rolled her palm around the purple head. I saw his stomach muscles twitch as she worked him faster, her hand eventually moving quickly enough that it looked blurry to me. He gasped, stifling a grunt, and I watched as the head of his cock swelled in size by half, and then he shot his white cum into the air. I could see the muscles behind his scrotum pulsing, another jet of semen bursting forth with each spasm. Finally, after a dozen shots, each one progressively less voluminous, he was done.

He sat up. His stomach and legs covered in his own fluids. He looked around for something to wipe himself off with, but the woman was having none of it.

"Hey, you can deal with being covered in jizz. We did. At least this is your own. Now, get over there and eat her pussy."

She pulled on his cock to get him moving, and then reached over and stripped me of my towel, throwing it across the room out of his reach. I didn't think I'd be ready for any more sex that night but watching his huge cock erupting had a libidinous effect on me. I was genuinely insatiable that night. I played along with the woman's directions and opened my legs to him, ready to receive his mouth.

He was good. Not as good as the woman, but he knew his way around a vagina. While he worked me down below, she climbed onto the bed and straddled me, her bald pussy an inch from my face. She didn't say anything. I stuck out my tongue, sliding it between her lips, and she dropped down onto me. She worked her hips forward and backward, fucking my face. I couldn't believe that I'd eaten my first pussy that night, and now was getting face-fucked by the same woman. By this time, the euphoric effects of the ecstasy were wearing off, and I still wanted her. Wanted to taste her, wanted to make her cum. Her juices flowed freely, running down my cheeks, her rhythm gaining momentum. I felt my own hips bucking, moving in the same tempo as hers.

Her thighs tensed up, and she started to cum. Just like before, I raised my hips and came at the same time. For the second time in my life, I squirted, covering poor Peter's face.

She climbed off me. "Fuck, you learn fast."

I smiled. "I've always been a quick study when I enjoy something."

The woman grabbed Peter by the cock again. "Oh yeah, he's ready for you." She turned to him. "Fuck her with that long cock."

I'd had two of the most powerful orgasms of my life that night, so I wasn't in desperate need of another, but I went along with it. I wasn't passing up on the longest cock I'd seen outside of porn. He climbed on the bed.

"You're okay with this?"

I spread my legs wide. "Give me your peter, Peter."

I heard the woman laugh, but then he was inside me, and I didn't hear much else. I'd never had anything, not even a dildo or vibrator, that deep inside my pussy. He started to pump his hips, and I swear he hit bottom on every stroke. It was uncomfortable.

"Hold on," I said. I pushed Peter off me and flipped over, sticking my ass in the air and spreading my legs. He mounted me again, and holy shit was this better. I mean, doggie style is basically reverse cowgirl without having to do the work, and that tool of his was running past all the right spots inside me.

I dropped from my elbows to my shoulders, optimizing his angle of entry, letting him drive my face into his pillow. His balls slapped against me, and I was drifting along on the edge of an orgasm for what seemed like forever. The woman had done me a huge favor making him cum beforehand because he lasted long enough to make me cum. I started pulsing, building pressure, climbing the wave, and just as I was about to cum, something felt different inside me. It clicked in my mind—the head of his cock just swelled. After watching him get jerked off by the woman, I knew what that meant, and I came, screaming into his pillow, clamping down so hard on that beautiful shaft that I thought I would rip it off. I felt him, like before, pumping over and over, filling me up with his cum. The poor boy was going to need a Gatorade.

Finally, he collapsed on top of me. I rolled sideways, and he stayed there, behind me. His cock was still in me, pulsing every few seconds, like aftershocks following an earthquake. I fell asleep like that, him inside me, his arm wrapped around me.

As I drifted off, I was satisfied completely, in a way I'd never felt before. And for the first time in a month, as Peter's semen dripped out of my tired pussy, I wasn't thinking about Phillip.

Breakfast Date

After drinking two bottles of wine at Gemma's house, I awoke with a hangover. I was going to go out and get a Hangover Special from Shakes Alive, but I remembered that I left my car at Gemma's, and Ubered home the night before. She offered to let me stay at her place, of course, but I was feeling a little self-conscious after spilling my darkest secrets to her. And worse yet, I knew there was more to the story she'd want to hear. A lot more.

I was debating taking another Uber to get my car when my phone buzzed. It was a text from Gemma.

My head's killing me. How's yours? If you tell me you're okay and going for a run, I'm going to kill myself. I need greasy diner food, stat!

I looked at the screen for a few seconds. Did I want to go out with Gemma today, after all the dirt-dishing I did last night? I'd have to see her at some point since I needed to get my car from her place, so I figured I'd just make it a date. I texted her back, teasing her.

"I just got back from a run. Was thinking of going to Shakes Alive for my whey protein and citrus hangover special."

The three dots danced under the message, then her reply came through.

I HATE you!

I laughed, and before I could reply, she added a line.

I'll come and get you. Address?

I sent her my address and rolled out of bed, peed, brushed my teeth, downed three ibuprofens, and tried to pick out something to wear. I opted for sweat shorts and a zip-up hoodie.

Gemma arrived a few minutes later, dressed similarly in comfy shorts and a Misfits t-shirt. "Tell me you didn't really go out for a run already!"

I laughed. "I'm lucky to be vertical. It's been a long time since I've drunk that much."

"Me too! I hardly remember anything from last night. Did we talk a lot, or did I imagine that?"

I perked up. Did she honestly not remember my sordid tale? Then she dashed my hopes.

"Just kidding, I remember everything. That's for making me think you went running today. Come on, let's go get one of your horrid sounding shakes."

I scowled, not happy that she joked about the one thing I was susceptible to. But, if I'd learned anything about her these last few days, it was that she was very direct. In a way, it was refreshing.

I told her where to go, and fifteen minutes later, we were sitting in a corner booth at my favorite shake stand, each of us enjoying one thousand calories of protein and fat-heavy recovery shake.

"I have to admit, this is pretty freaking good," Gemma said. "It tastes like orange cream soda! Reminds me of being a kid."

I nodded, sucking on my straw like it was paying me. When I came up for air, I pointed at the stenciled phrase painted on the wall at the rear of the building, above the restroom entrance.

I don't know if it's worth five dollars, but it's pretty f**king good. – Vincent Vega

"You and Vincent Vega agree," I said. "You'll be ready to go in a half hour after this. It's got vitamin B and C, whey protein, vanilla bean ice cream, and orange juice. It's seriously a miracle."

"We'll see. I'm a breakfast sausage and fried egg, side of Tabasco kind of recovery person. The grease soaks up all the toxins. At least, that's my theory."

"That does sound good but trust me on this."

"I will if you finish your story," she said, making sultry eyes at me.

"Ugh. You're a dog with a bone, Gemma."

"No, as I recall, you had the bone in you when we left off last night. That could have been the end of the story, except I had dreams about it last night. Dirty, wonderful dreams. I want more."

It was her turn to work her straw like it was her job. I looked around, and there was no one within earshot of us. "Okay, you're right. There's a little more from back in the day, and then some more recent developments. If I tell you that stuff, will you let it drop? I'm really not proud of it."

She reached over and squeezed my hand. "I'll never mention it again if that's what you want. And, I promise to give up my own secrets too. How does that sound?"

"Okay, that's a deal." I got ready to tell her the rest of the sordid college tale.

The Morning After, What a Pill!
Ten Years Ago

I woke up Saturday morning, still spooned with Peter. I looked around for the other woman, but she was gone. The only thing that indicated she'd even been there was my clothes, folded neatly in a pile on Peter's desk. My small purse and cell phone were next to them.

I realized I'd never gotten her name, and when I closed my eyes, I couldn't remember what she looked like. I supposed that might be an after-effect of the ecstasy or maybe the fact that I spent more time looking at her body than at her face. I admit I was disappointed she wasn't there.

I was also confused. I'd never been with a woman before, and as I knew from my session with Peter, I still loved getting the D.

But something felt different now. I was thinking about what her pussy tasted like and how much fun it was exploring each other's bodies. I wanted more of that. It was like a hidden universe that had been opened to me.

Peter stirred, and when I rolled over to face him, his cock was hard and poked into my stomach. Dammit, I wanted more of *that,* too.

I scooted down on the bed and took him into my mouth. Like I said, he was long but not very thick, so he fit in without trouble, but there was no way I was getting the whole thing inside. Just the first half of it would activate my gag reflex.

He moaned and moved his hips, but he wasn't awake yet. It's funny how men can be sound asleep, but their sex organ is fully functional. It really does have a mind of its own. I stroked his shaft, sucking on the top three or four inches, taking as much as I was able to into my mouth. I felt myself getting wet, so I sat up and squatted over him, working his cock back and forth between my lips, getting my juices on him, then started to lower myself. I dropped a few inches, then withdrew, then dropped down a little farther, each time getting more of his shaft wet and slippery. I finally had him all the way in.

I started working my hips forward and back, feeling him move inside me. It was thrilling, fucking him while he was asleep. I was taking advantage of a man without his consent, and though I was confident he would be okay with it, I felt a hint of that taboo electricity. The wave of pleasure started to build, and I moaned. My body fell forward, and I kept rocking my hips while I sucked and bit at his nipples.

That woke him up. He opened his eyes and registered a moment of alarm as his brain tried to catch him up on what was happening to his body. I was at the tipping point when he pinched my right nipple with one hand and tickled my clit with the other. That was it, I tumbled off the edge into my orgasm, pulsing and contracting, my pelvic muscles tensing and releasing.

I kept pumping away at him, and my orgasm stretched on. "Oh my god, cum in me!" I know I screamed it, but it sounded like it came from someone else. Someone with a raspy, lusty voice. I felt his tell, the swelling of his cock head, and braced myself for the torrent of cum he would unleash. I wasn't disappointed. Over and over, he shot his hot love juice into me, pulsating with each burst, and making me cum again.

I collapsed on top of him. "Holy Christ. I'm such a slut for you."

"You? I was you and your friend's bitch-boy last night. 'I'm jerking you off, now eat her out, now fuck her.' I just did whatever you all told me. And then I wake up, and you're using me as a sex toy!"

"And you loved every minute of it."

"Fuck, yes, I did. Where is your friend, anyway?"

I shrugged. "I don't know. I never met her before last night. I didn't even get her name."

His eyes went wide with surprise. "You're serious? You two seemed like a team, acting in concert with each other. You were so in sync, I just assumed you knew each other or were dating or something."

"Nope. I'd never even been with a woman before last night."

He was even more surprised by that revelation. "You're kidding me! You had me fooled."

"Me too! I didn't expect to like it. In fact, I only stayed because I'd had a fight with my friends, and if I left, it would have made them right. I couldn't give them the satisfaction."

"And you got some satisfaction of your own."

"Holy shit. Yes, I did. I'm probably going to walk funny for a week, but cumming, what, ten times? A dozen? Totally worth it."

"So... what now?"

I felt absently at my pussy, feeling the hot cum that slowly drained from me like lava. "Now, I go to the restroom, clean up, and head back to my apartment."

He had a look on his face that told me that's not what he meant.

"Oh, what now for us. Well, I'm single," as I said that, I realized Philip was all but gone from my mind. I flashed a wide grin. "So, I'm free to let you use that thing on me whenever you want." I grabbed his penis, which was about half the size limp as it was hard, and wiggled it, flicking drops of his cum all over him. "But I imagine you have someone who's laid claim to that thing already."

"No, actually, I'm between sexy nymphos right now, so I guess we should trade digits."

I gave him my number, and he started to provide me with his, but my phone was dead. "Just text me, and I'll get it when I get to a charger."

I slid out of his bed and walked naked down the hall to the bathroom, clothes under my arm, doing my best to channel the woman from last night. I shocked a couple of the boys I passed. One of them must have been in the basement because he said, "Last night was so fucking hot! You're a goddess!" I blushed, and thanked him, and sequestered myself in the bathroom for a few minutes, peeing and cleaning myself.

I went to put on my underwear, expecting my white panties with the red heart on them, but instead, the woman had left her teal-pink-and-white plaid G-string.

I'd never really liked G-strings, but I didn't want to walk home sans underwear, so I slipped them on. I was surprised that I was a little turned on, knowing she left these for me—I assumed as a reminder of our night together. There could be no other reason. I mean, she would never have confused my panties for hers. It felt like she took mine as a trophy. I felt a tingle as the thin strip of fabric passed between my legs and deep between my cheeks.

I finished getting dressed and made a semblance of something out of my hair. I returned to Peter's room, where he was just lying naked on the bed with a hard cock.

"Dammit, that's not fair!" I exclaimed.

"Sorry, but this is your fault. If you weren't hot, and..."

"DTF? I really can't. I have to work this afternoon." I spotted a bottle of lotion on his desk. "Tell you what, I'll take care of you, but you owe me one!"

I worked him up and down, the lotion providing the lubrication I needed to make quick work of him. His head rolled back, and he moaned, "Oh, fuuuuck!" I saw the signal and cupped my hand over him while he came again. His hips bucked into the air. A full load of cum cascaded down on his stomach and pubic mound, running down the gap between his leg and scrotum. He wasn't grossed out by his own cum, which was good, because if I had my way, there'd be a lot more of it to contend with soon.

I kissed him and left his room. "Gotta go. Talk to you soon."

The trip through the frat house was part celebrity welcome, and part walk of shame.

One kid didn't even have the courtesy to say hello. He just looked up from his phone and said: "Hey, are you going to come back and fuck more of us next week?"

I didn't answer, but I knew my face was red. The next couple of guys didn't seem to recognize me, and then I ran into Boomer. "How are you doing? You really went for it last night. That was legendary."

"Uh, thanks, I guess."

"Seriously, you're welcome. I don't mean that in a creepy way, but it was a fucking epic night. Are you leaving? You need a ride home?"

I debated it for a second. It would be a ten- to fifteen-minute walk, and my pussy was swollen. Though I had joked about it with Peter, it was uncomfortable to walk. "Sure, that'd be great!"

"Cool, let me go grab my keys!"

He disappeared for a minute, returning with keys in hand. He led me outside to an orange Jeep with a soft top and no doors. It coughed into life, and I gave him the name of the apartment complex. IIe pulled out of the frat's parking lot and turned left. As he drove, he made his motives clear. "So, listen, I was serious. Your performance will go down in history. It was the best thing I've ever been a part of. It was so crazy getting to bang you while you ate that other chick out. I'll remember last night for the rest of my life."

"That's great," I said. I didn't like where this was going. The term "unintended consequences" ran through my head.

"You should give me your number."

"Why?"

"So, we can hook up again. You know, keep the legend alive."

"I don't think so." It was puzzling to me that Peter could be part of this same crew, and yet so different from them.

"Why not? I mean, you already fucked me once last night. Why not hit this again? I know you liked it."

We pulled into the apartment complex. My building was on the other side, but I wasn't going to send him any closer to where I lived. "Right here is good," I said. "Thanks for the ride!"

"Whatever. You know, your legend will live on anyway. The video already has over five thousand views."

I stopped halfway out of the Jeep. "What video?"

"It's on all the sites. 'Party Girls Take Dick and Eat Pussy.' You should look it up. It was five stars last I saw."

I got out of the Jeep and started running for my apartment. I had no idea they were filming it, but I suppose I shouldn't have been surprised. Everyone with a smartphone had a video camera.

When I got to the apartment, Kelly was beyond pissed and screamed at me the second I walked in. "I can't believe what a whore you are!"

I stopped in the doorway. I assumed she had seen the video.

Sheila walked out of the kitchen. Her face was sad rather than angry. She looked disappointed. "Seriously, Darce, what were you thinking?"

I got defensive. "Hey, you're the assholes who dosed me with ecstasy! You're the ones who kept telling me to get laid."

Kelly spun her tablet around and showed me the screen. The video was paused, the frame showing me, on all fours, with my head turned toward a guy who was doing me from behind. A Captain America shield tattoo was visible on his arm. It was Todd. "Not only did you fuck half the Sig Om house, but you fucked the man I explicitly told you I wanted to get with—while eating out a *girl* like a fucking lesbo! And you let them film your face, you idiot slut! Your

75

life is fucking over. I'm sending this link to everyone you know. Starting with your parents."

I didn't know what to say. Should I try to calm her down? Should I go on the offensive? What was my move here? "Listen, Kel..."

"Don't 'listen, Kel' me, you slutty whore! Your life is over."

I knew what I had to do. I walked past my roommates and went to my room, got my car keys, and walked back out.

"Where the fuck do you think you're going to run off to?" Kelly demanded.

"The hospital. I've been drugged and taken advantage of. I need to get the blood test done before the drug leaves my system. Everyone on that video will go to jail, as will the people who gave me the drugs against my will. Maybe everyone I know will think I'm a whore, but you'll all be thinking it from prison, and I'll be free to eat all the lesbian pussy I want!"

Kelly smirked. "I didn't drug you. Nothing will happen to me."

"Hey!" Sheila protested. "It was your idea! You're not going to sell me out!" She turned to me. "Darce, I don't care what you did! I once sucked a guy's cock for ten dollars! I'm a *real* whore! Don't do this to me!"

Jesus Christ, she just opened her vault. I reminded myself to avoid relying on Sheila in the future. She'd fold under the slightest pressure. Outwardly, I just smiled. I locked eyes with Kelly. "You know, Charles Manson never actually killed anyone, but he's still in prison for life for suggesting other people do it. It sounds to me like you two have some things to discuss. I'll leave you to it."

I left and got a blood test at the urgent care center. The tech who took my blood was an attractive ruby-lipped young woman whose appearance leaned toward Goth. She smelled like clove and roses and had tattoos trying to escape her short sleeves. I remembered a saying I'd heard from a friend last year when all the freshmen—boys and girls—were rushing out to get inked. *"If she gets the ink, she'll take your dink."* Was that true? Were tattooed women more promiscuous? If so, I should have a full-body tat after last night. As she affixed a label to the tube of blood, I found myself wondering if she was waxed clean, or kept a puff of hair above her lips, or was just full bush under her scrubs.

What was I doing? I was dealing with the aftermath of an ill-advised night of whoring, and I was mentally undressing the first woman I interacted with—while getting blood drawn to check for illicit drugs I'd been dosed with. What was happening to me?

"You should really fill out a police report," the tech said, crashing my sexual thoughts into the ground and setting them on fire.

I just wanted some leverage to preserve what little of my reputation might be salvageable, not bring the police into this. "No, it's not like that. I just want to know what I was given. There's no need to involve the police."

She frowned at me. I could tell she was thinking about getting the cops involved anyway.

"Seriously," I said. "I was dosed with ecstasy, and I had a great time. I just want to know for sure that's what it was. That's all."

"Whatever. It's your co-pay. We should have the results this afternoon." She ripped a form off a clipboard and handed it to me. I took it to the front desk and paid my fifteen dollars and went home.

Sheila and Kelly were sitting in the living room when I walked in. Sheila looked like she'd been crying, and Kelly was still pouting, her face getting sourer as I walked by.

"What did they say?" Sheila asked.

"We'll know this afternoon. I hope you haven't done anything rash, Kelly, because the health center was super keen on getting the cops involved. I held them off—for now." I continued to my room without listening to anything else either of them had to say. I would go confront them once the test results came back.

I fired up my laptop, and I checked my email. Kelly had forwarded me the link early that morning, about an hour before I got home. It was in an email she received from one of the Sigma Omega members, and he got it from a secret Facebook group the frat guys were in. The only positive I could find was that the guys at the frat didn't seem to know my name.

Hey Kelly – you missed a wild time last night. That friend you brought really enjoyed herself though... and six of the brothers and some random chick Boomer brought for us. Check out who was first in line, the engine of the train. I told you he was no good for you. Sorry to show you this, but I thought you needed to know. I'm here if you need to talk. – JT Parr

I hated those "I thought you needed to know" people. They always said that when they were telling you something that was going to be hurtful, and in my experience, it was because there was something they wanted to gain. Clearly, JT Parr wanted to hook up with Kelly and had no problem selling Todd (and me) down the river to do it. Hell, Todd was probably in on that scheme. The brothers were thick as thieves about this stuff and were perhaps playing off one another to get the other one laid. Dammit, what was I thinking about, getting mixed up with a frat?

My brain vouched for me. *You weren't yourself last night. You were under the influence of drugs. You would never have done this otherwise.*

I let that thought bounce around my head for a few seconds. My brain was right—I never would have done what I did if I hadn't been on ecstasy. But I was a willing participant. I also had a lot of sex *after* the ecstasy had worn off, including letting that woman sit on my face. So, no, it wasn't just the drugs that made me do it. I would own my decisions.

I held my breath for a moment and clicked on the link.

The video was shot so you couldn't see any of the faces of the guys—the dim lighting helped mask them, and the camera they used must not have been high quality. I didn't care, I just wanted to see the woman's face. Unfortunately, she was in shadow, and the cameraman kept panning down to our chests and groins as we writhed on each other in the chair. Once, I saw her profile, but it wasn't enough for me to be able to recognize her if I saw her on campus.

I plugged in my headphones and scrolled forward to the point where I got on my hands and knees and started to service the mystery woman. Watching myself with my face in her crotch gave me the quickening. That was me on the screen, eating pussy. If I wasn't convinced it had happened, there it was in grainy low-def on my laptop screen.

Todd moved in behind me and slid a finger into my pussy, and I whipped my head around. That was the image Kelly had frozen on her tablet when I walked in this morning. Over the noise and laughter of the frat brats, I heard myself say, "Fuck me!"

Todd dropped his pants and fell to his knees, aiming his dart at my bullseye. He hit the mark, going deeper with each thrust until he was pounding me at full speed. When he came, he moaned, "Oh, my god!" He went through his vinegar strokes, pulled out of me, and backed out of the frame. No one moved for a moment, and the woman shouted, "Fuck her!"

Boomer hopped into the frame; well, hopped into *me*, really, dropping to his knees and driving his cock into my hole in one movement. I hit pause for a moment. His penis was perhaps five inches long, and that was being generous. I hit play again. He pumped me for about thirty seconds before convulsing with his orgasm, spilling his seed inside me.

Really, Boomer. That's the kind of performance you think I want to "hit" again? You're a sad little man.

Onscreen, I shouted, "Next!" Another brother hopped into place and slid into me.

I let my hand drift down to my groin. My pussy lips were still swollen and a little sore, but I fingered myself, and the feelings of pleasure quickly overrode the discomfort. I moaned a little, feeling my hips move of their own accord, my rhythm picking up speed. Onscreen, brother number five was inside me, and the woman in the chair had her legs pulled up to the sides of her head, giving me complete access to her pussy.

Number five got up, and number six got on. He lasted longer than everyone, other than Todd. He shuddered, cumming inside my pussy. I came and the woman came.

Reliving the triple orgasm sent me over the edge, and I came hard, clenching and pulsing, feeling the rush of juices into my underwear.

Correction: *her* underwear. My impulse was to change them, but I decided to leave them on. I felt more confident with a piece of *her* on me. It was like armor. Pussy armor.

My phone came to life on its charger, and the text notifications started buzzing. I only answered one—from Peter to let him know I got his number and for him to call me some time—and read another. There were several more from Kelly and Sheila, which I didn't bother to read. The last one was the clinic confirming they'd found ecstasy (MDMA, or 3,4 methylenedioxymethamphetamine) in my system. I forwarded the text to Kelly and Sheila.

I went out to the living room where Kelly and Sheila were looking at their phones. I walked over to them and took a seat on the couch. "Well? What's it going to be?"

"Jesus, Darcy, you still reek of sex," Kelly said.

"That's because I just watched the video and masturbated, Kelly. I couldn't help it; it was so hot watching the replay." Her face seethed with anger. This wasn't going to help me keep her from sending the link to my parents. In all honesty, they were the only ones I cared about seeing it, so I backpedaled. "I'm sorry, that was unnecessary and mean—"

"And gross."

"Oh, it's not like we don't hear you doing it in the shower, Kelly." That drew a laugh from Sheila, who got a reproachful glare from Kelly. "Look, I'm sorry. For the record, I had no idea who Todd was when he started hitting on me. And when he showed up behind me in the basement, well, I wasn't thinking about anything but... my own carnal desires. I know you like him, Kelly, and I'm sorry. But he doesn't feel the same way, clearly."

"Not now that you fucked him, that's for sure."

"He doesn't care about me, either, Kelly. He'll have his cock in someone else in that basement next weekend. Probably before then."

She looked at her phone. "Are you going back there? Are you going to do that again?" She pointed at her screen. "JT says you're all they're talking about today, about how into it you were, and how can they get you back down there."

"I'm not planning on it. That was kind of a one-off situation. I just went for it, and without the ecstasy on board, I never would have done it. But everything felt so good, I just wanted more and more and more. I didn't do anything out of spite, and I have no desire to do it again. Please believe me."

"Well, Sheila and I talked, and I won't send the link to anyone, but you have to promise to never go to the police," Kelly said. "I told JT to delete the link from their group and to tell the brothers to stop forwarding it. I can ask him to take the video down completely if you want. He said he would."

I pondered this for a minute. I was sure more than one of the brothers already had downloaded the video, so it would never truly go away. And, if I made a big deal out of it and forced them to remove it, I'd just be ensuring that they'd keep posting it elsewhere just to be dicks. It was grainy enough footage; I didn't think anyone could recognize me unless they knew in advance that it was me. Better to leave it where it was and let the buzz die down. In another week, they'd post a new video, and mine would be forgotten.

I relayed my logic to the girls.

Sheila nodded. "I think that's the right way to go. You're right, once it's on the Internet, it never really goes away. And men are like infants; if you make something forbidden, that's all they want to do."

"Tell JT the video stays up, but I don't want them promoting it. It's for Sig Om use only. Maybe if they feel special, they'll honor the request."

Kelly nodded. "I'll tell him."

So, I lived in an uneasy peace with my two roommates for the rest of the semester. A few weeks after the big event, Sheila confessed to me, after many drinks, that she had masturbated to the video several times and wanted to know what it was like to be with a woman. We waited for a weekend when Kelly was gone, and I let her roll in the hay with me. We had a lot of fun—she called it "a vacation from herself"—but it wasn't as intense as it was with the mystery woman, who I never saw again. After that weekend, Sheila would sneak into my room from time to time, even when Kelly was home to get some girl time. I was always happy to oblige. She was enthusiastic when she went down on me, and grateful when I did it to her. She's married and has kids now. When I lived in California, she came out on business, and we went and got dinner, then went to my apartment and fucked. That was after she was married, but before the kids, so I'm her dirty little secret. I still chat online with her every now and then. She's turned out to be a pretty decent person.

Kelly went back to the frat the next weekend and tried to get into the basement so she could fuck Todd, but they didn't have a party like the one I attended. She ended up making a video with JT, which of course, he uploaded to the porn sites. While she pretended she didn't like having it out there, she wouldn't stop talking about how many views it had, and what her percent rating was. She got super pissed when she found out the frat had monetized the account, and they were getting paid every time someone watched one of the videos they posted, but she wasn't getting a cut. I lost touch with her when the semester ended, and we all moved out of the apartment. She unfriended and blocked me on Facebook, and I've never gone searching for her.

Peter and I dated for about three weeks, but eventually, he just couldn't handle the hazing from his frat brothers. They all started calling him Mills, like Brad Pitt's character in the movie Seven. First, because he was the seventh guy to fuck me that night, and second because they kept saying, "Who's in her box?" playing on the line at the end of that movie. They did it no matter the situation. Once he and I were in the student center on campus and Boomer walked past, practically shouting, "Who's in her box? Mills! Who's in her box? I was! I was in there before you, Mills!"

I replied, "Yeah, you were, Boomer, all four inches for an entire thirty seconds. Hardly worth shouting about." The other SigOms with him cracked up.

Of course, that pissed him off, and his taunting of Peter turned mean. It got to the point that Peter was ready to fight him, but that would have gotten him tossed out of the frat. In the end, it was bros before hoes.

He said the nonstop hazing was too much for him. I was initially upset, but I didn't blame him. I stared into the future, and I could see the two of us, in our thirties, married, and the brothers would still be calling him Mills. They'd probably show the video at his bachelor party. He was right—it wasn't going to work between us. It was too bad because I really did enjoy that big cock of his. He ruined me for normal-sized guys for a while—though if they're girthy, that makes a difference.

At the end of the semester, I left town. I'd already been accepted at another school on the coast, and I put this place in my rearview for almost a decade before moving back.

I never saw Peter again—until one day at the supermarket a couple of months ago.

Video Replay

Gemma sat behind her empty shake glass with her mouth hanging open. "That's the craziest story I've ever heard! I thought you were a warrior goddess before, but you handled your business like a pro!"

I looked across the table at her. "None of this really bothers you? It doesn't make you think less of me?"

"Why should it? It's in the past. It brought you here. And like I said, I have my own twisted tales. Anyone worth knowing has something troublesome in their past. So, what happened when you saw Peter a couple of months ago? Did he recognize you? How did he look? Did he get fat? I bet he got fat."

"We'll go through that another time, okay? I don't have the energy for it right now."

Disappointment flashed across her face, but then her expression brightened. "Well, that gives me something to look forward to. I hope you take this the right way, but I can't wait to hear more about this. You're fascinating."

I took a chance and leaned forward. "Well, until then, can I show you something?"

She nodded. "Of course!"

I looked around to ensure we were still alone and stuck my thumbs in the waistband of my shorts and wiggled my hips, pulling them down past my knees, and spread my legs wide open.

Gemma's eyes grew wide. I think she thought I was showing her my bald beaver. She leaned over, wearing a huge grin. Under the table, she was greeted by a teal-pink-and-white plaid G-string.

She sat back up. "Shut *up*! You still have her G-string? Ten years later?"

I wiggled my hips as I pulled my shorts back up. "Yep. Every time I see it, it reminds me of a wild night where I did what I wanted without regard for what anyone's opinion was. A night I was truly free. It makes me feel like I can do anything I want. I only wear it on special occasions, so it's lasted forever. You're going to think I'm a sap, but I keep hoping that one day, I'll be able to give it back to her."

Gemma smiled. "Can you imagine? What if she still has yours? With the heart on it?"

"Oh, I can't imagine that she does. I wasn't her first conquest. I bet she moved to the next person right away."

"I don't know. She took your heart, literally. You must have made an impression."

"Well, not enough of one that she tried to find me afterward. But that's okay—who knows what she's like now? I have that one, deliciously erotic night of hedonism to look back on. In my mind, she'll always be perfect, even if the fallout afterward sucked for a while. Like you said, it made me who I am today."

We threw our empty shake cups in the trash, and Gemma drove me back to her house so I could pick up my car. She asked what I was doing the next day, specifically if I was going to the gym or not. I told her I'd have to check my mail and see what new projects had come in, and I'd get back to her.

When I got back to my house, I grabbed my laptop and plugged the HDMI cable into the TV. I scrolled around and found the folder with *the video* in it. The frat guys had stayed up the remainder of that night, ten years ago, editing two hours-worth of footage down to a forty-minute video. That was crazy long for amateur porn, especially by today's standards, but it was action-packed. Most videos I had seen were between five and fifteen minutes. Given what I had been through recently, watching this would probably be a bad idea, but I hadn't watched it in a long time. I double-clicked it and stretched out.

It started with me in the chair with the woman. It was uncanny the way the shadows seemed to follow her face, keeping me from getting a good look. I scrolled ahead a little bit, to where she undid my top and pulled it down.

Good grief, I was so *young* in this video. And soft. I paused it and took my shirt and bra off. Even though I was ten years older than in the video, in my opinion, my tits looked better now. They were bigger, for one thing—36C versus 34B. I was slender back in college, but I had zero muscle tone. Now I was not just thin, but I was muscular. I doubt I could have bench pressed half my body weight when that video was made, and now I was pushing one hundred fifty-five pounds. I was squatting one eighty-five, and I was able to do thirty pull-ups and fifty pushups. Modern me would kick college me's ass. My hair was a mess back then too. I'd tried dying it blonde, away from my natural red, and that looked horrible, so I went back to red, but it came out almost orange. So, I went brown. The result was a mousy mess. Now I was back to my natural burgundy shade, which, again, in my humble opinion, looked fantastic.

Onscreen, college me was squirting all over the mystery woman. I felt a tingle in my nethers. Well, I knew how this was going to end. I stripped out of the rest of my clothes and teased myself along for a few minutes, then scrolled ahead to the finale, the triple orgasm. Even though the woman onscreen was a lesser version of myself, I still paid her tribute and made the ending a quadruple orgasm. I turned on some chillout music and closed my eyes for just a moment, and promptly fell asleep, naked, on the couch. It was the best quality sleep I'd had in a long time.

Busted

For the next few days, both Gemma and I were busy with work, and our schedules were mixed up, so we kept missing each other at the gym, but we texted each other a few times a day, usually just to tell each other random thoughts. It was really nice to have someone to do that with again. I didn't feel alone anymore. Friday afternoon, I got a text from her.

I need to finish a financial risk assessment for a client tonight. Fun Friday night! :-(Circuit training tomorrow? Lunch after?

Not that I had anything on my calendar, anyway, but I was purposely keeping things clear in case she wanted to do something. I enjoyed the few days we'd spent hanging out. Even though it wasn't the most comfortable topic, in the end, I had fun telling her about my past. I got a vicarious thrill at her amazement in the face of my—how should I put it?—*nonspecific* sexuality. I walked both sides of the line, but my desires had a tendency, like over the last couple of months, to get me into trouble, and Gemma seemed enthralled by my escapades. If I were honest with myself, her reactions gave me a thrill, too. She seemed turned on by the whole thing, and I liked turning her on. I had already decided I would tell her everything she wanted to know about me, and there was plenty more to say. I replied to her text.

"Sounds perfect. Ten?"

Nine thirty. I need to put in some extra work after this week.

"See you then!"

I read a book that night, had a glass of wine, and went to bed early. I knew that Gemma could go harder on the treadmill than I could—though I'd been stepping up my game since I met her—so if that was any indication, I imagined she'd be hard to keep up with on the circuit too.

Gemma's idea of a circuit was different from mine. I usually broke my strength days into opposing muscle groups, like chest and back, or arms and shoulders. Gemma wanted to do everything. Squats, bench press, curls, lat pull-downs, you name it. I was pleased though—I could bench more than she could, and I could curl more too. She had me beat on lats and tricep pull-downs, and we repped the same weight on squats. After we went through all the stations she wanted to hit, we climbed on treadmills. This time, we ran side by side.

I set mine to seven and a half miles per hour to match Gemma. I was glad I'd been pushing myself because I was able to keep up with her for fifteen minutes. I reached up to cut my speed to seven, but Gemma thought I was increasing it, so she bumped hers up to eight. There was no way I could hang with that speed, so I just focused on my form and my breathing. Before I knew it, our thirty minutes were up, and we slowed to a walk for an extra five to cool down.

We wiped the machines down and went to the locker room. I grabbed my bag from my locker and was heading toward the showers when Gemma grabbed my hand. I instinctively laced my fingers in hers before I realized it. She didn't seem to mind. For a second, I thought she wanted to shower together, and I felt a thrill run through me.

"Let's go back to my place. We can shower there. I have the stuff to fix for lunch."

On the drive over, I kept wondering what she meant by "We can shower there." I had that flash of a thought that she wanted to shower together at the gym, which would have been *crazy*—but hot as hell— and I was a little disappointed that wasn't the case. But going back to her place—was she going to ask me to join her in the shower there? I would absolutely jump at that chance. I'd already had dreams about what I'd like to do to her body. But I couldn't assume that was what she intended.

I was smart to not assume. Gemma poured me a glass of wine and showered first, then prepared lunch while I basked in her enormous shower. It felt like I was naked outdoors in a rainstorm, with the overhead showerheads washing the sweat from my body. I used her scented soap and lathered up as much of my body as I could reach. I was one big scrubbing bubble, and I loved it. After spending five minutes in that deluxe shower, the one I had at home would feel like being in a seedy hotel.

Speaking of my shower, I eyed the handheld unit on the far wall. It was identical to mine, and I couldn't resist the temptation. I pulled it from its base and used it to rinse clean, then, as if this wasn't my intention all along, I pushed it against my pussy. I felt the thrill of two dozen high-pressure streams of water touching my most sensitive flesh all at once. I knew this was inappropriate because it wasn't my house, and Gemma hadn't made any overt overtures toward me, but the image of the two of us showering together that had formed in my head while I followed Gemma to her house had built a need within me.

I reached down with my other hand and rubbed my clit, then slipped two fingers inside, moving them in and out, faster and faster. I wiggled the showerhead, sending the streams of water to different locations. I brushed my thumb over my button, and my knees buckled. I could feel an orgasm building.

I fell, more than sat, on the bench, one hand working the showerhead, the other hand working my flesh. Everything else faded away, and I came in a rush. I heard myself cry out, but I couldn't stop it if I tried—and I didn't want to, at least not at that moment.

The wave passed, and I opened my eyes. I thought I saw a shadow moving away from the bathroom entrance. Did Gemma come to check on me? Was I that loud? I felt embarrassed, like how I imagined it would feel getting caught by my parents.

I stood, and washed my hair last, letting the rainfall rinse the shampoo out, and I dried off with the towel Gemma left out for me. After I got dressed, I went out to the kitchen to join her.

"Isn't that shower amazing?" Gemma asked as she handed me a glass of water. "I could spend half a day in there when I get stressed. I just love it."

"It was wonderful," I agreed, taking a sip from the glass. *More than you know,* my brain added.

"It's way better than showering at the gym. Besides, you can't really masturbate at the gym. People look at you funny if you're loud."

I coughed, spitting up water. Gemma *did* catch me! It was funny—even though I'd told her every detail about a college orgy I wantonly participated in, the thought of her finding me playing with myself was somehow more mortifying.

"What?" she asked. "I told you I've done some things. Everyone does it. It's no big deal but scream 'oh fuck' in the shower at the gym while you cum, and all the women give you attitude. It's partly why I come home to shower."

Maybe she *hadn't* seen me.

"Like, I heard you cumming just now, and I was like, 'Yeah, she knows not to waste an opportunity.' I don't know why people get so uptight about it."

I gulped. Busted. It was time to change the subject. "So, uh, what's for lunch?"

"Turkey pesto avocado wraps and Tapatio Doritos. Don't worry, the tortillas are low carb. The Doritos, however, are not. But dammit, they're good! And while we're changing the subject away from auto-erotic pleasures, you have more of your story to tell me."

Gemma didn't miss anything. "Right. Why do I feel like I'm at a deposition every time we meet? The subject always turns to my sordid past."

"Because, Darcy, you fascinate me. When I first saw you at the gym, I knew we would be good friends. I'm way more interested in you than in talking about myself. You seem to need to unburden yourself, and I'm cheaper than a therapist. Plus, it's like a real-life erotica audiobook for me. Are those enough reasons? Seriously, you don't have to tell me anything you don't want to. We can just eat in silence like a couple of psychopaths."

I laughed. "Okay, well, let me first say, these Doritos are insanely good. I'm glad we worked an extra half hour today because that bag is going down."

She raised her eyebrows suggestively. "I have another one in the pantry."

"Well, I guess I'm going on a long run tomorrow then. So, where did I leave off?"

"You said you saw Peter a couple of months ago, and you showed me your lucky panties."

"Okay. Well, I had just moved back to town, and I was going around, getting the lay of the land. What gym was closest and most affordable, what supermarket is the best, stuff like that. It had been a decade since I lived here, and a lot of things had really changed.

"But some had stayed exactly the same too."

Re-Pete
Three Months Ago

I was in the produce aisle at Kroger's, looking for fresh cilantro, when I heard a man call my name. I turned and looked, and there he was. Peter.

He looked good. A lot of guys get out of school, get a desk job, and get fat. But not Peter. He looked older—because he was—but his basic features had held together well. He'd grown up but hadn't *aged,* if that makes sense. Even his hairline was hanging on—a little higher than it was before, but the forehead was not quite a five-head.

"Peter!" I exclaimed. I'd been here a week with no real contact with anyone, so I was excited to see a familiar face. "I had no idea you were still in town! You look great!"

"You do too!" His eyes worked me up and down. I was glad I'd fixed my hair and put on a little bit of makeup before I went out. I was in shorts and a tank top but had a running jacket tied around my waist because it was still spring, and I never knew when it would turn chilly.

I took his compliment in stride. "Thanks. I try to stay in shape."

"Seriously, you're one of those people that's gotten better looking as you've gotten older. You must spend all your time at the gym."

I laughed, but it was true. I did spend a dozen or more hours working out every week. "Peter, you act like we're fifty or something. I'm not even thirty yet. I'm supposed to look good. I'm just hitting my prime."

"True, I suppose. So, are you back for good, or just visiting?"

"Who would I visit here? I'm back for good. Or, back for now, anyway." I spotted the ring on his finger. "Peter Olsen, you got married!"

He blushed a little bit and held up his hand, looking at the ring like, *How the fuck did this thing get on there?* "Uh, yeah, I did. Three years ago, last month. We have a twenty-month-old daughter."

"Wow, good for you." Then, I couldn't help it—the words were out of my mouth before I knew I'd said them. "Are you going to teach her to stay out of fraternity basements?"

"Oh, man, Darcy. I was hoping that wouldn't come up." He seemed genuinely uncomfortable with the topic.

I reached out and touched his arm. God, I was flirting with him! "How could it not, Peter? It's the whole reason I met you. And for what it's worth, I don't regret it. I had fun that night, and I had fun the short time we were together."

"Yeah... I'm sorry about that too. It was pretty weak of me to end it over what the other guys thought. I've often looked back on that with regret."

He seemed like he'd become a—dare I say it—*good guy*. "I get it. Peer pressure is a mother. And seriously, I don't bear any ill will over you ending it. I was planning on leaving town at the end of that semester anyway. It would have been nice to ride Peter's peter for another few weeks, but hey, we don't always get what we want."

"True that. Listen, it's really good to see you, Darcy. I mean that. You look like you're doing well, and that makes me happy. I'd love to catch up some time."

Before I could stop myself, I blurted out, "I'm free right now. Why don't we grab a coffee?"

He pulled out his phone and looked at it. "Yeah, you know, I don't have anything on my calendar for the rest of the day. I just needed to get diapers before heading home. I can hang for a few."

I left my cart where it was since I hadn't gone very far down my list. Peter bought the diapers he'd come in for, and I followed him in his Range Rover to a Java Jungle. Even though the place was close to empty, we grabbed a table in the back. I suppose he didn't want anyone seeing him with a woman who wasn't his wife.

We covered the usual "catch up" topics. I told Peter about finishing school in California, how living near the beach in San Diego got me into working out, how I hated working for a corporation and started doing side gigs on a temp site, and I turned that into a successful business that allowed me to go where I wanted, when I wanted.

For his part, he finished his business degree and ended up buying his dad's insurance practice. He met his wife, Kimberly, toward the end of his senior year. They dated on and off for a couple of years and lived together for three before getting married. Kimberly was pregnant six months later, and for now, was a stay-at-home mom.

"Is she hot? She'd better be, or I'm going to get jealous."

He pulled out his phone, opened a Facebook album, and handed it over to me. She had short blonde hair and skin so white she made me look Hispanic. She had broad shoulders, small breasts, and a tiny waist. She looked like a gymnast. Her smile pushed her cheeks up and revealed a set of brilliant white teeth. I had a wicked thought about her and pushed it out of my head. "Wow, Peter, she's a hottie! I can see why you put a ring on it! Well done, old man!"

"Thanks. Kim was a cheerleader in college, so..."

"So, she must be kinda petite and... acrobatic?" Again, my mind was wandering toward the gutter.

"She's five foot four, one-thirty. The last ten pounds of baby weight has been stubborn. God, she'd kill me if she knew I told you her weight."

"Jesus, Peter, it's not like she's obese or something. Relax. So how does she handle Peter's peter? I mean, you have a kid, so we know the pieces fit, but that's a long pipe for a shallow well."

He squirmed with this line of conversation, clearly uncomfortable with me talking about his penis. "She likes it just fine," he said. "It's just... we've been in kind of a rut since the baby came."

I wasn't expecting the conversation to take that turn. "I'm sorry, Peter—"

"Pete, please."

"Okay, Pete. I didn't mean to pry or bring up a sore subject. I was just—I don't know. Busting your balls? Sorry, I probably shouldn't mention your balls, either."

He laughed, which made me feel a little bit better. "No, it's okay. I shouldn't dump that on you, so it's my bad. It's just…"

"It feels good to open up to someone?"

"Yes! Exactly. And, given our history, it's not like we have any secrets, you know?"

I smiled. "Yes, Pete, I know exactly what you mean. I have some skeletons deep in my closet, and you were there when I put them there."

"And you're very easy to talk to. You never judge. I feel a little guilty because…"

"All you've been thinking about for the last twenty minutes is how much fun we had in bed?"

"Is that what you're thinking about?"

"No! Unless—that's what you're thinking. Then yes. I want you inside me."

Ten minutes later, Pete was cumming inside me on my entry rug. We hadn't even bothered to close the door before he had my shorts pulled down and his long, hard cock pushing its way between my wet pussy lips. We were feral, rutting like animals, and it was beyond incredible. He rolled off me, and I put my head on his chest, letting my hands run over his stomach and watching it twitch.

"Holy shit," he said. Those were the first words either of us said since arriving at my house. "I can't believe that just happened."

I felt the familiar river of cum seeping out of me. "How long has it been?"

"Three months, give or take. And a few months before that."

"You have to give it time, Pete. A baby fucks with a woman's hormones like you would not believe. She'll come back to you."

"Oh, I know, it's not like we're on the verge of divorce or anything. But this felt... right. I don't know. I got semi-hard the moment I saw you in the store. All those old, familiar feelings came flooding back. I'm just trying to justify it. Fuck! I just cheated on my wife!"

"Pete, I won't tell her, and you for sure better not. Besides—it's not like you've done this before, right? Cheating, I mean. And this doesn't really count—I mean, you've already hit this pussy. Your number didn't go up. So technically, it's not cheating."

He was drawing circles around my nipples, making them stand at attention. "Nice try, Darcy. It's not okay, and we can't do this again."

I sighed. "I know. This was fun, and I needed some deep dicking, but it was a bad idea."

At three o'clock the next day, he knocked on my door, and at three-thirty, I was screaming, thrusting my hips into the air and cumming in his face. I will say he and I were very compatible in bed. We knew all the right moves, like a quarterback and wide receiver reunited after a decade spent with other teams.

"This doesn't count, either," he said. "You didn't get off yesterday, so I owed you this one."

I agreed. "Yeah, it's really just a continuation of what we started on the floor of my entryway. That was basically foreplay."

"Right. But no more after this."

"Agreed."

We lay on my bed, his face shiny with my juices, my pussy happy as could be.

"Same time tomorrow?" he asked.

"Sounds good."

The next day I answered the door naked. We didn't even make it out of the entryway before he lifted me up and sat me on his cock. He carried me like that to my bedroom, where he threw me onto my bed and took me from behind. That day, we both came.

The day after that, I again answered his knock naked, and he had his erection out, glancing around furtively when I opened the door. I grabbed his divining rod and pulled him inside, climbing onto him and pushing that shaft inside me while he let his pants fall to the ground and penguin-walked to the couch. I sat astride him, thrusting my hips in the cowgirl position, shoving my tits in his face. His orgasm practically blew me off him. He was still cumming in me while the first salvo was dripping out.

It went on like this for a couple of weeks. The weekends were hopelessly long and interminable, and each weekday Pete would come over at lunch or at the end of the day. We'd pleasure each other, then he'd clean up and leave. It was almost like a business transaction, but we were having the time of our lives. It was the first time in more than a year that I was getting laid daily, and I forgot how satisfying that is.

After the first few weeks, we slowed it down. It wasn't an intentional thing. One day I had a late meeting, another he had new clients he was signing policies with. Our daily trysts became thrice weekly, then twice a week, and then he got serious about ending it. He told me he thought Kimberly was getting suspicious. She was asking a lot of questions, and despite our torrid affair, he really did love her. I told him I respected that but left an open invitation if he needed to talk—or do anything else. I would give myself to him whenever he wanted.

I thought that would be the end of it until a week later, when I ran into the whole family at Home Depot.

Super Tasty

Y ou always leave me wanting more," Gemma said. "That's the mark of a good entertainer." She looked at her watch. "Shoot, it's almost three. I have some work I need to do. Promise me you'll tell me the rest later!"

"Of course, I will. I can't seem to say no to you. Why don't you come over for a run tomorrow morning, and we'll have breakfast after?"

"Perfect."

We ended up not going for that run. I was in the mood for sushi that night, and something in the jalapeno tuna rolls disagreed with me. I was up half the night throwing up, and in the morning, I was in no shape to run. I texted Gemma to tell her I wasn't going to make it.

Around eleven, my doorbell rang. I knew that I looked like someone who had been throwing up for several hours, and even though I wasn't expecting anyone, I answered the door. It was Gemma, dressed in her running attire—with a giant probiotic shake from Shakes Alive!

I was so happy I almost cried. "Oh my god, you're a lifesaver! I was just wondering what I was going to eat for lunch, but nothing I have here sounds good. This is perfect! Thank you so much!"

I wrapped her in a long hug, lingering long enough to get my emotions in check, and invited her in. She looked around the entryway, and I saw a smile spread over her face.

"What?" I asked. I realized she'd never been inside my house before, and I was worried she was laughing at my décor.

"I was just wondering if I got that semen light from CSI, how much of this entryway would light up?"

"Fuck you," I said, laughing as the words left my mouth. I looked around at the floor and walls. "Like, so much. It would look like someone was murdered here." I pointed toward the couch. "And there." I pointed to the hallway leading to my bedroom. "And there. A lot of murder scenes in this place."

"Yeah, you murdered some dick!"

"Come on, CSI Amante, let me show you the rest of the house."

I showed her the living room, where I'd been lying on the couch under a blanket, binging *Supernatural* on Netflix. I grabbed a bottle of water for her from the fridge as we passed through the kitchen. Then we walked down the hall, where I showed her my office, which was fortunately relatively clean. A Jack-and-Jill bathroom connected it and the guest bedroom, which was *not* clean. There were boxes and miscellaneous things piled up on the bed and in the closet. "I don't have a lot of guests," I explained. I could tell the mess bothered her analyst's mind, but she didn't say anything.

We walked to the master bedroom. I stepped in front of the door. "You cannot say anything about the state of this room. I was not expecting company today."

"What, do you think I'm conducting an inspection? Besides, I know not everyone is as anal as me about things. I think it's because I'm in finance, so everything must be perfect in my work, and that carries over to my personal life. I wish I could be messier."

She motioned for me to move aside, so I let her pass. She glanced around at my unmade queen bed, the mess of charging cables on my nightstand, and the many dirty clothes near—not in—my hamper but offered no commentary. She peeked inside my bathroom, which was very small and simple compared to hers. She flashed me a wicked grin. "Hey, you have the same handheld showerhead as me!"

"Yes, I noticed that too," I said, remembering that she caught me masturbating with hers. "Obviously."

"I like it, Darcy! This is a great place. I wish I would have gotten a three-bedroom... but that bathroom was such a deal maker. I don't know if I would have found one in my price range anyway."

"Well, I had a motivated seller. I had to basically re-do the whole backyard because they had a neurotic lab that liked to dig and eat sprinkler heads. I had to patch drywall in my office, and the place needed a lot of updates on the appliances. Plus, the privy in the guest bath wasn't working, so I had to fix that. I was out of money to hire other people by then, so I had to fix that one myself."

"Oh, yeah, you offered to help with mine. Maybe you can go to Home Depot with me later this week and help me figure out what I need to do."

"I'd be glad to. I do know my way around Home Depot. In fact, that's where my story picks up. You want to adjourn to the living room?"

Gemma smiled that gorgeous, toothy smile of hers. "You know I want to hear more, but only if you're up for it. I know you don't feel good, and I only intended to bring you the shake and go."

"Oh shit, the shake! It's melting!" I grabbed her hand and led her to the living room, snatching the shake from the dining table on the way. I took a big pull from the large-diameter straw. "Mmmm, still cold and super tasty! You are an angel of mercy!"

I settled on the couch, and Gemma took a seat in the cushioned chair opposite me. She kicked off her shoes and pulled her knees up to her chest, looking like a little kid about to hear someone read a story to her. Which, I guess, is what I was doing. "So, speaking of super tasty and Home Depot, guess who I ran into there one fine Sunday afternoon?"

Home Depot
Six Weeks Ago

I was walking down the central aisle at the rear of the store, looking for the plumbing aisle, when I saw Peter and a woman who I assumed was his wife pushing a cart toward me. I'd seen the picture of his wife on his phone, but she was way more attractive in person, even holding their toddler. She looked older, more mature, but sexier. Her short blond hair was the right style for her. I don't think many women can wear short hair and make it look good, but on her it was perfect. Her breasts were more prominent than in the picture, too, but that was probably owed to the pregnancy. She *glowed* as she walked along with a gymnast's grace. I'd had fleeting, dirty thoughts about her when Pete showed me her picture but seeing her in person was different. I felt a tingle inside, and a hunger stirred that I hadn't felt in a long time.

Peter saw me, and I could tell he was hit by a sensation of panic. I wanted to head him off before he said something stupid.

"Peter!" I exclaimed. I walked up and gave him a hug. The look on his face was pure deer-in-the-headlights. I'd be lying if I said I didn't enjoy putting him on the spot a little bit. I was in control here, and he was freaking out.

"Pete?" his wife asked, suspicion heavy in her voice. "Who's this?"

I turned to her. "I'm sorry! I'm Darcy Ford. I knew Peter back in college, and I ran into him at the Kroger's the other day. You must be Kimberly? He showed me your picture and told me all about you and your beautiful daughter. From that picture, I thought you were a hottie, but I must say, you are way prettier in person!" I turned my head a little toward Peter. "Way to go, Peter!"

"Pete," he said, catching on to my act. "I go by Pete now, just for the record."

Kimberly relaxed a little and extended her hand. She clearly liked that, according to me, the first thing he did when he met me was to shove her picture in my face. "And I go by Kim. It's good to meet you, Darcy. How is it that Pete's never mentioned you before?" She looked sideways at Pete, but I answered instead.

"Well, I transferred to a different school after my second year, and we hadn't seen each other in, gosh, like, ten years. I just moved back a few weeks ago, so you'll probably run into me again, especially if you come here a lot. My house needs a lot of work." Their daughter reached a hand toward me and made that grabby-grabby motion that kids do. "Isn't she precious! Can I hold her?"

Kim paused a second, then passed the little girl over. She really was a cutie—I wasn't faking that part. I took her and addressed her as one addresses all non-verbal cute things. I did baby talk. "What's your name, cutie-patootie-pie?"

The girl laughed and said, "Pop pop pop. Boppa pop."

"Her name's Rebecca," Kim said.

"Well, Rebecca, you're going to have to work on your pronunciation. Pop pop pop boppa pop isn't quite how you say your name."

She drooled on herself and said, "Poopa poo!" then she made a farting noise and blew spit bubbles all over herself.

"I bet you learned that from your daddy!"

The little girl laughed, then made the grabby motion toward Kim, so I passed her back. "Oh, you guys, she's adorable!"

Kim beamed. "Thanks. We think so, but don't all parents?"

"You're the exceptions that are right."

"Well," Pete said, trying to extricate them from this awkward situation. "We've got some stuff we need to get to before this afternoon, so..."

"Oh, of course! I'm sorry, I didn't mean to hold you up." I noticed Kim's phone was about to fall out of a side pocket on her big bag. "Oh, watch out, this is going to fall!"

I grabbed her phone, and when I did, I hit the home button. The phone didn't have a passcode. I took a risk, opened the text app, and started typing.

"Um, hello? What are you doing?" Kim demanded.

I typed a few more characters and hit send. My phone buzzed in my pocket. "I texted my phone. Now you have my number. I don't really know anyone in town, so if you ever want to get coffee, or whatever, just hit me up!" I leaned in close and handed the phone back to her. I lowered my voice, making it huskier than usual. "I'd love to get to know you better."

She blushed, her red cheeks standing out against her porcelain skin as she put her phone away. Pete was already wheeling the cart down the aisle. "Good to see you, Darcy," he said over his shoulder.

Kim looked at me and smiled, the flush fading from her face. "It, um, it was nice to Darcy you. To meet you! It was nice to meet you, Darcy." She hustled to catch up with Pete.

I went on about my business, got the parts I needed, and was working on fixing my toilet that evening when I heard my phone buzz with a text alert.

Hi Darcy, this is Kim Olsen, Pete's wife. I'm running a couple of late errands. Can I bring you a coffee?

What the fuck? I gave her my number like five hours ago, and she wants to come over? I knew I'd dangled some bait, but I didn't really expect her to take it, and certainly not to contact me this soon. On the other hand, she was hot, and she wanted to come to my house, and she made my loins tingle. What could go wrong? I texted her back.

"That would be awesome! I like lattes if you're going somewhere that has them. Otherwise, black coffee is fine."

The three dots danced for a few seconds.

Is a McLatte okay?

"Perfect." I gave her my address and went back to work on the toilet.

Thirty minutes later, the doorbell rang. I went out to answer it, and there was Kim, changed out of her Home Depot shopping outfit, and dressed super cute in black capris and a pink top that let just a sliver of her belly show. She had open-toed shoes with a thick, two-inch heel that brought her almost up to my barefoot height.

By comparison, I was a slob. I was wearing a pair of gray sweat shorts and an old, ratty tank top that had seen a few too many wash cycles. It had a hole in the stomach, and the sides were stretched out, showing my side from my shoulder to just past the bottom of my ribcage. It made me self-conscious that I wasn't wearing a bra. "I'm sorry," I said. "I look horrible. I was working on the bathroom and lost track of time. I should go change."

She extended the latte to me. "No, don't bother! I know I surprised you by texting so soon, but I just had some things I wanted to talk to you about before they drive me crazy. And you look great, by the way. I wish my working-around-the-house look were as striking as yours."

I felt my face get warm. "Well, that's a lie, but I'll take it. Come in, Kim, have a seat."

We sat in the living room, and I took a sip of the latte. It was actually pretty good. I was pleasantly surprised. "So, what's on your mind?"

"Okay. I'm just going to get to it. When you were in college, did you and Pete used to date?"

I felt a trap. Kim had likely already had this conversation with Peter—Pete, I mean—and I had no idea what he would have said. I decided the truth was probably the best and easiest way to go. If he lied about our relationship, that was on him. "Yeah, we did. For about three weeks."

"I thought so. He acted really nervous when you walked up to us in the store. I thought he was going to have a panic attack!"

I laughed. "Yeah, guys are dumb. Worlds colliding, and all that."

"Were you two... intimate?"

Again, I decided truth was the best, but I dressed it down a little to take the focus off Pete. "Kim, if I dated someone in college, we were going to be intimate. In fact, that's why he broke up with me."

That surprised her. "Wait—*Pete* broke up with *you?* But... you're gorgeous!"

I felt my face heat up again. "It's true. I had a bit of a reputation, well deserved, I'm afraid. I think Pete's friends even teased him about it, and ultimately, I just wasn't what he was looking for."

I could tell from her face that she was both relieved and confused.

"Does it bother you that Pete and I were together?"

"No. I mean, I know he's been with other women. But he's bccn acting really weird lately. Ever since the baby came, he's been more distant. And then over the last few weeks, he's been out of the office at lunch a lot and working late. I was actually wondering if he was cheating on me."

I leaned forward. "Cheating? Because he eats lunch and works late sometimes?"

"I know, it sounds stupid when I say it out loud. He was just suddenly less affectionate, more distant. God, I can't believe I'm telling you all this. We literally just met each other today."

I leaned back, and when I did, I felt my left breast slip partially out of the side of my tank top. The nipple was just exposed, and I felt it hardening in the open air. I was feeling a little devilish, so I decided to see what Kim would do. I left it where it was, acting like I didn't notice. "I don't know, Kim. Like I said, guys are dumb. Maybe he's still just a little weirded out about you giving birth or something. I have friends that told me their husbands took a while to get back to seeing them as sexual beings." I'd read that in a *Cosmo* in my gynecologist's waiting room a few weeks prior while I waited for my annual exam. I couldn't believe I actually found a conversational use for a *Cosmo* article!

"Yeah, maybe. Um, Darcy?" She gestured at my tit hanging from the side of my tank, but never averted her eyes. "You're, uh, hanging out there."

I feigned embarrassment. "Oh, my god! You must think I'm horrid! I knew I should have put on a bra. I just hate wearing them. I used to have B-cups, and I could get away with it, but they've grown, and well, you saw what can happen."

"Well... um, they look like they're holding up well, from what I saw. You say they've gotten bigger?"

"Yeah, I think it's because of the birth control I switched to a few years ago. It's one of the side effects. All things considered, that's a good one to get, I guess. But whatever the cause, they're larger than they used to be. Certainly, larger than Pete would remember."

She laughed an uneasy laugh. "Well, at least I've seen something that Pete hasn't! That would kill him if he knew! When you said they've grown, I thought you maybe got a boob job. It was so—perfect."

"Well, thank you. I work out a lot to try and keep things tight. I can assure you they're real." I paused and then decided to go for it. "You want to feel them and see for yourself? Now, that would *really* drive Pete crazy!"

She just stared at me for a second. "Can I tell you a secret?"

I leaned forward, purposely pinning the right side of my tank under my arm, allowing my left breast to break free again, but keeping it hidden behind my left arm. "You bet. Who would I tell, anyway? I only know you and Pete, and I, for sure, won't tell him."

She licked her lips and took a sip from her coffee. "When you said you wanted to get to know me better in the store today, it sounded... sexual."

I leaned back, breast exposed, but didn't say anything.

She stared directly at my nipple but didn't say a word about it this time. "You're not denying it. So, you *did* mean it that way. I was thinking about it all morning and this afternoon. Every time I replayed it in my mind, I felt a little charge run through me, just like I did when you said it. I mean, when I was on the cheer team in school, some of the girls were, um, playing for the other team. But they never hit on me. That thrill I felt when you said that—it's something I've never felt before. It had me totally flummoxed! I even, um..."

She trailed off, staring at my nipple. "You what, Kim? You can tell me."

Her words came out in a rush. "I pleasured myself in the shower, thinking about it before I went out. Thinking about you!"

Her face turned bright red. She leaned back in her chair and finally looked away from my breast. She buried her face behind her hands. "Oh my god, I must sound like a lunatic to you. I've known you for less than a day, and I'm telling you about my husband not having sex with me and that I play with myself in the shower thinking about random women. Next, I'll tell you that I made up my errands just so I had an excuse to see you again."

"Did you? Make them up?"

"Who has errands to run on a Sunday night, Darcy? Of course, I made it up. Oh god, I should just go before I embarrass myself any further." She started to get up, but I stopped her.

"Kim, I told you I had a reputation in college. A well-earned one. You thinking of me while you masturbate isn't weird. I'm flattered that a gorgeous woman like you would think of me that way."

"You're kind," she said. She was staring at my breast again. She licked her lips. I knew I had her on the hook. She pointed at my exposed flesh. "You're doing that on purpose."

I crossed my arms, lifted the tank over my head, and tossed it aside. Her mouth fell open, and I felt my face and chest get warm with a flush. "Go for it," I said. "I've wanted you to touch me ever since I saw your picture on Pete's phone."

She leaned across the coffee table and grabbed a breast in each hand, holding them like she was assessing which one weighed more. My nipples grew impossibly hard, and she dragged a thumb over each one. A fire ignited in my pussy, and an involuntary gasp escaped my throat, totally surprising both of us. It snapped her out of her reverie.

"I need to go!" she said, dropping my breasts and practically sprinting for the door.

I grabbed my tank and held it over my chest. "Kim—"

"No, I'm going. Thank you for the talking to. For talking about Pete. My husband!" And like that, she was gone.

I returned to the couch. That was, without a doubt, one of the strangest, most exciting few minutes of my life. Well, of the previous nine and a half, anyway. I looked at my phone, tempted to text her, but decided to let her run. Following my fishing analogy, she needed some line to tire herself out so I could reel her in. My pussy still tingled, thinking about this game we suddenly found ourselves playing. I was tempted to play with myself, but I didn't give in to the urge. Not yet. I closed my eyes, thinking about her hands on me, how heavy and full my breasts felt as she hefted them, how exquisite her soft, delicate touch was on my body. I wanted more of that.

I was about to give in and pleasure myself when my phone buzzed.

Darcy, I'm sorry I freaked out. I shouldn't have. You were so sweet after what I told you I did in the shower. So nice to make me not feel like a weirdo, and to offer yourself to me like you did. I didn't mean to run away. I just... I don't know. I reacted badly.

I typed out a reply. "Don't worry about it. I was probably a bit too aggressive. I'm generally not like that, but I was serious, from the moment I saw your photo, I've felt drawn to you. Then, when I saw you in the store... I found you irresistibly alluring. Whether I want to be or not, I'm attracted to you."

The three dots danced.

I've never been called alluring before.

So... I did it again.

"Did what?"

What I did in the shower. I pulled over a mile from your house and pulled my pants down, and I did it. I think a homeless guy saw me. I'm so ashamed... embarrassed.

And excited.

I thought for a moment, then simply typed, "Holy shit!"

OMG! I can't believe I typed that! WTF is wrong with me? You have to delete this chat!

I set the phone down, slid my shorts off, put my feet on the coffee table, and reached down. I never get tired of that first touch. It's like powering on a computer. Everything lights up. I rolled my head back, amazed at how wet I still was from when she fondled my tits. I imagined her in her car, her capris pushed down to her knees, her hand rubbing her clit, her fingers sliding in and out of her pussy, and after she came and her senses returned, she saw a random guy peeking in her windows. It only took me two minutes to cum, my hips lifting, bucking at my fingers, my entire upper body in a flexed, crunch position, my stomach tightened, my pelvic muscles contracting and relaxing over and over. I pinched my nipples with my free hand and let loose with a scream as the wave crashed over me. I collapsed, panting on the couch.

My phone buzzed. I picked it up and saw several texts from Kim.

Darcy? Are you there?
Where'd you go?
RU there?

My god, this was so much more exciting than fucking Pete! I typed a reply. "I'm here. Had to play with myself real quick. You can't have all the fun. I was thinking of you touching my tits, and I had to do it."

Nothing happened for a moment, then the three dots danced.

Holy shit.

I laughed.

I'm going running at six tomorrow morning. Join me?

I smiled. Kim wasn't fooling around here. Time to reel her in. I stretched out naked on the couch and typed three words in reply.

"I'll be there."

Sharing The Same Brain

H oly shit," Gemma said. "That's exactly the right phrase. You're lucky I didn't start masturbating while you were telling that story."

I didn't react right away.

"Great, you're imagining it now, aren't you?"

I blushed because I *was* picturing her playing with herself. "No, I—I just couldn't think of a witty comeback. You caught me flat-footed."

"So, I have to ask again—you're not messing with me, right? This is all true?"

"Every word. Why would I make this up?"

"I don't know. To see me get all twisted up over it? You should write a book."

"Yeah, right."

"Seriously. This stuff is *hot*."

"Well, I'm not going to write a book about my sex life. Besides, you don't know how this story ends."

"Well, I know you're still alive, so nobody boils your bunny, and I got to meet the most interesting friend I've ever had. So, there's that. But I totally understand why you reacted the way you did that first day in the coffee shop when I used your phone to text mine. And for the record, I don't blame you. That would have freaked me out, too, so, retroactively, I'm sorry."

"Apology accepted in arrears. Now, change of subject. Are you going to the gym tomorrow?"

"Yes, but I have to go early. I have meetings in the afternoon."

"Bummer, I can't meet early. I have a call with a team in Europe at six."

She patted my knee. "No worries, I'll get a hold of you sometime later this week and see what you're up to. But now I have to go. I have some stuff to do this afternoon."

I walked her to the door and thanked her again for the shake. It had me feeling a hundred and ten percent better. She gave me a hug, and I watched her hips sway as she walked to her car, her shapely ass looking like perfection in her running shorts. I saw my neighbor across the street pause what he was doing and ogle her as she got into her car and drove away. I think he mouthed "wow" before returning to the project in his garage. Or, maybe I imagined it because that's what I was thinking.

I returned to the living room and lay back down on the couch, thinking about the next few "chapters" of the story. Gemma was right, they were pretty hot. In the few weeks between things ending with Pete and Kim, and meeting Gemma, I was truly alone. I had relived the events that were coming up in this tale several times, using them to pleasure myself when I felt low. Maybe there *could* be a book in there somewhere. If I got myself off thinking about my adventures, possibly others would if they read about them. I was a writer, after all. I pushed that thought out of my head and let my fingers drift down to my pussy, feeling the hair that was starting to grow back. I'd need to go get waxed soon.

I absently tickled and teased my lips, spreading them apart and feeling the wetness between them. I was starting to breathe hard when my phone buzzed.

I stopped a mile from your house.

No way. Gemma did not pull over, masturbate, and text me in an attempt to re-enact the scene from my story. Or did she?

If this is where Kim stopped, someone for sure could have seen her. There are several condos on the hill that can see right into my car. And several people walking by on the sidewalk. They can see in here too. Kim couldn't have picked a worse place from a privacy perspective to stop and rub one out. She must have had it bad for you!

I realized I still had my hand in my pants. I started working my fingers inside my pussy, rubbing my clit with my thumb. I managed to type a reply to Gemma with my other hand.

"And what are you doing now?"

I felt my hips bucking. How did I go from just casually touching myself in peace and quiet to full-on masturbation while texting with my friend? Jesus, I must have pent-up needs, because it seemed like I was touching myself every ten minutes.

Wouldn't you like to know? ;-)

I dropped my phone as I came, my pelvic muscles contracting over and over. I withdrew my hand from my pants, the sweet smell of my cum drifting to my nostrils. I was panting, and my heart was racing.

Holy shit.

I searched the floor for my phone, grabbed it, and started typing.

"Come over for dinner tomorrow night. 5:30. Just bring yourself."

It wasn't a request. I didn't ask if Gemma was free. I demanded her presence. She replied right away.

Let's make it five.

The next morning, I had my meeting with the Europeans at six AM, then went for a long hard run. After a shower and a few more hours of work, I went

133

shopping, and by four-thirty, I had everything in motion for dinner.

The bell rang at four fifty-eight. I smiled and answered it, inviting Gemma inside. She held out a brown bag, which caused me to frown. "I said you didn't need to bring anything."

She reached inside and pulled out a bottle of Tequila Blanca. "Tonight's a margarita night," she said. "With dinner, or after, we're having margs."

I started laughing, taking the bottle from her, and walking to the kitchen.

"What?" she asked, following me. "I didn't see any tequila in your kitchen when I was here yesterday. I can't come to dinner empty handed! It's not polite."

I set the bottle on the counter, next to an identical bottle of Tequila Blanca I'd picked up earlier in the day. "Second time we've bought the exact same thing. One more time and I'm going to start freaking out."

"Okay, on the count of three, how do you like your margs—frozen or on the rocks? One, two, three! Rocks!"

"Frozen!"

"Well, there you go, we don't share a brain after all. Frozen it is—your house, your rules."

Gemma grabbed the blender and went to work on the margs while I finished frying the taco shells and cooking the ground beef, mixing in the taco spices and fresh cilantro. Gemma sniffed the air like a hound. "Wow, I hope these taste as good as they smell."

I put the shells on a tray next to bowls of shredded cheddar cheese, chopped lettuce, and diced tomatoes. When the beef was done, I placed the pan on a hot pad in between our plates.

We assembled our tacos, and with the first crunch, Gemma moaned with delight. "Oh my god," she said through a mouthful, "These are amazing!"

"It's the freshly fried shells. Premade shells taste like cardboard. You'll be ruined for tacos anywhere else now. You're welcome."

"That just means you have to be my taco supplier from now on. God, these are good!"

After dinner, we retired to the living room with a fresh pitcher of margaritas.

Gemma sat on the left end of the couch, and I sat on the right. I swung my feet up and turned to face her. She did the same, leaning against one of my big pillows and rubbed her belly. "If I died now, I'd be okay with that. I could have eaten a thousand of those. You just pulled ahead in the cooking competition."

I smiled. "I didn't know we were in a competition."

"We are now. I don't know how I'm going to top those tacos."

"Maybe you can't," I teased.

"I still have a few tricks up my sleeve."

I sipped my margarita, careful to keep the blended slush from resting on the roof of my mouth. I hated brain freezes. "Well, it's funny that you mention competition because there's a bit of that in my next chapter. Get comfortable."

She leaned forward in anticipation, her face bright and attentive.

"So, Kim left in a rush, then texted me that she was overcome with lust and had to stop on the way home to take care of that situation, then invited me to go running the next morning. Well, there was no way I wasn't going to see what the morning would bring. I was so excited I could barely sleep. At five till six the next day, I pulled up in front of Kim's house."

Now We're Even
Four Weeks Ago

I parked on the street in front of Kim and Pete's house. Pete was doing well for them, that was certain. I had gathered that much seeing him in his Range Rover the day we reconnected, but their home was nestled in the foothills on a decent-sized piece of land in a swanky neighborhood. My Mini convertible wasn't out of place but was a low-end vehicle compared to what I saw as I drove there.

The house itself was a two-story affair, and from the street, it looked like each level was bigger than my entire house. Selling insurance must be a lucrative gig.

I had just shut the car door when Kim came out, pushing a running stroller in front of her. I waved and walked up their driveway to meet her.

"Hi!" she said. "I hope you don't mind; we'll do a couple of slow miles to warm up, and I'll drop Becca at daycare. Then we can really hit it. I'm almost back to my pre-baby shape, and I need someone to push me."

"Sounds perfect. Lead the way!"

I let her set the pace as we wound our way through the neighborhood and onto an eight-foot-wide concrete path. The pre-dawn light was getting brighter, and as we approached the daycare center, the sun broke over the horizon, bathing Kim's back in an orange glow. Her ass was perfectly shaped and highlighted by the morning sun, and I realized that, like me, she had long legs for her height.

We went through the front door and were greeted by a young but stern-looking woman. When she recognized Kim, she smiled. "Hi, Kim! I was so happy to see Becca on the schedule for today! She's such a delight, and the regular kids love her. It always makes their day when she's here."

Kim pulled her daughter out of the stroller and kissed the sleepy child on her cheek. "You be good today, okay? And have fun with the other kiddos!"

Another woman came, took Kim's bag containing all her baby-related gear, and led Becca inside the central part of the building. The woman behind the desk turned her attention to me, looking me up and down. I wasn't sure, but I think she scowled at my running shorts and sports bra. In her defense, the outfit did leave me with a lot of skin showing compared to Kim's mid-length shorts and long-sleeved running jacket. The morning was chilly, but I always warm up after the first half mile, so if the starting temperature is over fifty degrees, no coat. It was forty-eight, according to the thermometer in my car, which I figured was close enough.

"Who's this?" the woman asked.

Kim was watching her daughter as she went through the door and disappeared into the center of the building. "Oh, sorry. Karen, this is my friend Darcy. She's training with me today." She turned to me. "Karen owns this place. She's a lifesaver. When you have kids, I can't recommend her enough."

I took Karen's extended hand. "Good to meet you."

"You too. Aren't you cold?"

I looked down at my bare legs and midriff. "No, not really. This is actually my ideal running temperature."

"Well, it has to be a lot warmer for me to go out without a coat. You must be tough. Go easy on my Kim today."

Kim laughed. "Thanks for looking out for me, Karen. I need Darcy to push me, though. Can I leave the stroller here for the day?"

"Of course. You two have a good workout."

Kim turned toward me and ushered me out the door. "She likes you," she said as we started running. "She normally doesn't engage with strangers."

"She seems protective and judgmental."

"Only at first. Come on, there's a great trail over here."

Kim led me up a trail that wound up the side of the first of the foothills. I wasn't used to running hills, and my legs were protesting. By the time we hit the top, I was out of breath. Kim slowed and turned to me, also breathing hard, and tied her jacket around her waist. "I've never made it to the top in one shot before. There's an African proverb I read once—if you want to go fast, go alone. If you want to go far, go together. This is what I meant by 'I need you to push me.'"

"I meant to ask you; how did you know I ran?"

"You don't get a body like yours by walking on a Stairmaster. That ass, maybe, but not the rest."

It made sense. Also, it thrilled me that Kim had been checking out my *entire* body, not just thinking about my tits. She started running again, and the trail wound in and out of trees along the ridge of the hill, then switch-backed its way into a valley, over a bridge, and eventually connected back with the bike trail that snaked its way through her neighborhood. It was just after eight-thirty, and we'd logged eleven miles with a couple thousand feet in elevation gain and loss. I would feel that in the morning, for sure.

We walked for a few minutes to cool down. I was curious where this was going to lead, but I was ready for about anything. I also didn't want to freak Kim out again like I'd done yesterday afternoon, so I was going to let her make the first move.

"So, Darcy... Pete's gone to work by now, so I have the house to myself. You want to come in for a coffee?"

"Sure! I have time for a cup or two, but then I should get home to shower. I do have some work to do this afternoon."

She took my baited statement and ran with it. "Do you want to shower here? We have like, three guestrooms with showers that never get used. It could save you some time."

I felt devious. Either Kim was easy to lead where I wanted her to go, or she was very good at acting like she was being led. Either way, showering at her place sounded like it could lead somewhere fun. "Sure, that sounds great!"

As we approached her house, I stopped by my car and grabbed my bag from the back. She looked at it suspiciously. "You came with a bag prepared?"

Of course, I came prepared, but I made it sound more innocent. "I keep a change of clothes in my car in case of any accidents while I'm out and about. It's a trick I learned from an old boss. He kept a clean shirt in his office in case he spilled food on himself during the day and kept a full change in his car in case he ever got stuck somewhere overnight."

"That's actually smart. I should tell Pete to start doing that. I mean, the shirt at the office thing. He'd better not get stuck overnight somewhere in town—he's only fifteen minutes away!"

She hung her jacket on a hook by the interior garage door. "So, coffee first, or shower first?"

I took a discrete whiff of my armpit, and I caught her doing the same. In unison, we said, "Shower!"

She gave me a quick tour of the house and set me up in a guest room next to the master. I washed quickly, eager to see what would happen next. I wrapped the oversized, fluffy towel around my body, tucking it in above my breasts, and stepped out of the shower. I was startled to see Kim in the guest room, wearing a robe, hanging open, white high-cut panties, and no bra. Her assets were hidden behind the fabric of the gown, but her porcelain skin teased me from the top of her panties, over her toned stomach, through the shallow valley between her breasts and up to her slender neck. She looked delicious, and I wanted to run my lips and tongue over that path. She smiled, but her face turned bright red. She opened the robe and let it drop down to her elbows, leaving her perky breasts exposed to my hungry eyes.

She looked down at her tits and expressed some self-doubt about their size. "You would think the pregnancy would have done more for me, but believe it or not, they are bigger than they used to be."

"They're, um, they're perfect for your size." I stammered like a twelve-year-old boy seeing boobs for the first time. She was really getting to me.

"Well, I guess this makes us even since I saw yours and everything. Oh, but I guess you should... touch them? Then we'll be even."

I said I would wait for her to make the first move, and this was it and then some. "You're sure you want me to?"

She gulped as I stalked closer to her. I felt like a predator, and based on her expression, she felt like my prey. With both of us barefoot, I was four inches taller than her, so she looked up at me as I drew near.

"No, I'm not sure. But I want you to do it anyway. I... need you to push me."

I reached out and touched her shoulders, letting my hands slide along her collar bones. Her breathing quickened. My fingers traced a path down to her tits. After drawing a circle around each one with my fingernails, I wrapped my hands around them. Her skin broke out into goosebumps, and I felt her nipples grow stiff under my palms. Her heartbeat quickened, beating a furious pace, thumping against her ribs.

"Your heart is going to beat out of your chest."

"I've never been so scared and thrilled at the same time. I want you to ravage me, and I want to run away. We shouldn't be doing this! I'm not gay!"

I bent down and took a nipple into my mouth, sucking on it and biting gently, then I did the same to the other breast. Kim's breath was coming in gasps. I leaned close and whispered into her ear. "Don't label it and just listen to your body. The idea excites you. Just go with it."

She gulped. "O-okay."

I shrugged out of my towel, standing in front of her in all my glory. Her eyes grew wide, and I put a hand behind her head, pulling her down to my tits. I practically forced a nipple into her mouth. At first, she resisted, but after a second, I felt her relax, and then she sucked on both of my nipples, alternating between them, pinching and rolling her fingers on the one she wasn't sucking. I moaned a little, and I felt her body get stiff again.

"We're not even anymore. I'm ahead," I said, gesturing to my naked lower half.

"I guess, um, we should do something about that?" she said more as a question than a statement. I tugged at her robe. She dropped her arms to her side and let it fall to the floor.

I pushed her onto the guest bed and climbed on top of her. She locked eyes with me, and I wasn't sure if I saw desire or terror. I know I was feeling pure, high-octane lust. I hadn't felt like this since...

The night in the frat house. Only this time, I wasn't nineteen years old, I wasn't high on ecstasy, we had no audience, and I wasn't the pupil. And I was just as excited as I was that night.

I kissed her full on the lips, gently at first. It took her a second to respond while she reconciled it in her head. Her mouth was warm and wet, and her tongue was elusive, but I found it with mine. I leaned on an elbow and ran my other hand along her body, from her neck, over her tits, down her taut stomach, and across her panties, which made her twitch with an involuntary spasm. I continued down her thigh as far as I could reach, then lightly reversed that path with my fingertips barely contacting her milky skin. Her stomach jumped and spasmed, and her arms and chest raised goosebumps again. I kept gently running my hands over her, and she started kissing me back.

She was hesitant at first, but then her tongue sprang to life, probing my mouth, circling mine. She bit my lip—which I fucking *love*. When she did that, I felt the quickening surge through me, and my pussy tingled. I started spending more time on her stomach and thighs, and then I edged my fingers into the waistband of her panties. She moaned and lifted her hips ever so slightly. I found a crop of short hair—something I'd not felt on my own pussy since I started waxing after the night at the frat house.

I kept probing, finding her slit, and I ran a finger down its length. When I reached the bottom, I pressed harder, spreading her lips just enough to allow the tip of my finger inside. I worked it north, dragging it deeper as I went. She was wet, but by the time I reached the top and caressed her clit, she was flooded. I repeated this a couple of times, hearing her breath speed up. She stopped kissing me and buried her face in my neck, sucking on the flesh above my collarbone. She emitted a few quiet "oohs" and "uhs" as I continued to let my fingers do the walking.

I added a second finger to my motions, running it up and down her slit to get it lubricated with her juices, and I plunged them both inside her. She bit me in surprise and shrieked, "Oh, fuck!" I worked my fingers in and out for a few moments and

146

then withdrew my hand. She moaned again, and when I looked at her face, all traces of fear were gone. I was staring at one hundred percent lust. I kissed my way down her neck, sidetracking for each of her nipples, then proceeded south across the plain of her belly. I pushed her legs apart a little and felt another surge when she spread them wide for me. She looked so sexy, lying on the bed topless, her white panties showing a wet spot from her passion. I moved in between those toned legs, and hooked my fingers under her waistband, over each hip, and tugged, pulling her underwear down a couple of inches.

I've heard men talk about that moment when a woman lifts her hips, helping them take her panties off, and what a great moment that is. That's when they know she's going to let them in. When Kim lifted her hips, I felt that thrill. She was *into* it. Kim wanted everything I was going to give her. I seriously almost came when she did that.

She pulled her knees up to her chest, and I slid her panties off, throwing them on my towel. I put a hand on each knee and pushed them apart, exposing her wet, glistening pussy with its trimmed blond mane. I looked up at her, gauging her readiness.

"Do it, please," she begged. "Lord help me, I want this so bad."

I practically dove on her. My own lust had built to such a frenzy that I had become the beast devouring my prey. I licked her from stem to stern, my tongue just brushing her anus, then pressing harder and splitting her lips apart. I pushed my tongue inside her, then withdrew it and traced circles around her clit. She squealed, bucking her hips, driving her pussy into my face. I slid two fingers inside her again, working them in and out, my tongue dancing around her lips and clit like a ballerina. She moaned and grabbed a handful of my hair, not pushing my face into her, just seeking something to hang onto.

Her juices were flowing, making my entire hand wet. I extended my little finger and touched her anus, putting just a bit of pressure on it. She responded by raising her hips against it, and my finger slid inside.

With two fingers in her pussy, one in her ass, and my tongue writhing everywhere else, she came hard and fast, digging her nails into my shoulders, letting a scream loose, closing her legs around my head, and bucking like she had no control over her body. I kept working, dragging her orgasm out as long as I could, her moans tied to each pulse of her pelvic muscles. Finally, she could take no more and pushed my head away from her.

I slid up next to her and threw a leg over hers, pressing my bald, wet pussy against her hip. I kissed her stomach and her flush-reddened chest, sucking on each nipple again, then delivered a series of kisses to her neck and lips. Her breathing was finally slowing down.

She licked her lips and smiled at me. "Holy shit."

I grinned back. It was empowering to leave her spent with pleasure.

"I mean, holy fucking shit. Never," Kim gasped. "I've never cum like that."

"My first time with a woman was mind-blowing. It's a different orgasm than you get with a man. In some ways, it's a lot better. At least, that's my experience."

"Holy shit."

I used my fingertips to trace circles on her stomach.

"Darcy, even Pete's dick, never did that for me. And you know what it's like, right?"

"It was a long time ago," I lied, "but you don't forget a dick like that."

"Right? Holy shit, I'm still trembling." She raised herself to an elbow and looked at my pussy.

She reached out, and I eagerly opened my legs to her. She touched it, rubbing her whole hand on it, then pressing her middle finger between my lips and drawing her hand up to my clit.

I gasped, my body aching for more.

She raised her finger to her face and sniffed. "It smells just like mine," she said like it surprised her. She looked at the dew glistening on her fingertip, like someone trying to decide if something is edible. I suppressed a giggle when she licked her finger. "It's kind of sweet and bitter at once. It not what I expected."

I smiled. "You've never tasted yourself before?"

Her face turned red. "No! It... never occurred to me."

"My first time, I was surprised at how good it tasted. Frankly, if you ever had a man cum in your mouth, eating pussy is no big deal."

Kim laughed and reached over and stroked my face. "I came all over you."

"Heck yeah, you did. It was delicious. Glorious. You're amazing. You almost made me cum."

"Darcy..." the trepidation crept back into her voice.

"What is it?"

"I don't think I'm ready to, um, return the favor. I'm still processing what just happened to me. What I wanted to happen. What we just did goes against everything I was raised to believe. Please don't be mad."

I was disappointed, to be sure, but I wasn't going to try and pressure her. Besides, after the way she just came, I knew this wasn't the last time we'd be together. "That's okay," I said. "I came into this day with no expectations. I decided to just roll with it, no matter what did or didn't happen."

Relief washed over her. "Oh, my god, thank you! I can promise you; we'll do this again. Christ, I came so hard. No matter how much we do this, I'll think of this day for the rest of my life. I just need to work up to taking care of you. It's a big leap for me."

"Kim, it's okay. There's no rush and no pressure. I want your beautiful mouth on me as much as I've ever wanted anything, but I don't want to force it. I want you to want it too. Trust me, doing it out of desire versus obligation will make it way hotter for both of us."

She pulled my face to hers and kissed me. "I can't wait to..."

The front door slammed shut, and Kim sat bolt upright. "Fuck, what time is it?" she whispered, looking around for a clock. I spotted one on the dresser.

"Quarter after eleven."

"Oh, fuck, oh fuck, Pete's home for lunch. I was horny last night, as you know, and when I got home from your place after, uh, playing with myself, I gave him head for the first time in ages. Before the baby, we used to fuck at lunch all the time. He only comes home during the day if that's what he wants."

We heard his footsteps tromping toward the kitchen, and his voice boomed from the first floor. "Kim? Where are you?" She jumped up and put on her robe, tying it shut around her naked cheerleader's frame. "I'm going down there. I'm just telling him we ran and showered—separately! —and you're getting ready to leave. I'm sorry, I had no idea this would happen. I thought we'd have more time."

"Go," I said. "I'll come down in a minute. After I get dressed."

"Okay. Just leave your towel in the bathroom. I'll get it later." She took off, and I hurried to the bathroom. I whipped the yellow sundress out of my bag and slipped it over my head, not bothering with a bra or panties. I took a minute to fuss with my hair so it wouldn't look like I just got done fucking Pete's wife. Finally, I gave up and just pulled it into a ponytail. I slipped my feet into a pair of sandals, stuffed everything else in my bag, and headed to the stairs.

As I walked down, I saw Pete and Kim talking. She turned her head and said, "There she is now!"

I raised my hand to wave, and I almost dropped my bag. I scrambled for it, just grabbing the strap before it was out of reach, and yanked it back, bringing it back up to my shoulder. Unfortunately, the hasp caught on my dress, lifting the front of it up. I felt the breeze all the way up past my waist.

"Oh, dammit," I exclaimed, pushing it down. I couldn't believe I'd just flashed my beaver at Kim *and* Pete both. Maybe they hadn't seen it. Maybe the stair railing blocked their view.

The shocked look on Pete's face and lusty look on Kim's told me they'd seen everything I had to offer. I set the bag down and acted as if nothing had happened. "Hi, Peter. Pete, sorry."

"Uh, hi?" he said. It came out as a question.

I hugged Kim. "I loved that trail, Kim. It kicked my ass. We have to do it again sometime." She returned the embrace, dropping an arm to her side, keeping her body between it and Pete, and reached forward, grabbing my pussy through the dress, rubbing it a couple of times before letting go of me. I tried not to gasp.

"Absolutely!" she replied. "I really needed someone to push me to go farther than I have before. I loved every minute of it. I'll text you, and we can hit it again!"

"Great! See you soon. Bye, Pete."

"Yeah, see ya, Darce."

I bent down to grab my bag and saw the tell-tale shape of Peter's peter, rock hard, straining at his khakis. Kim was in for a treat.

I left, letting the screen door close, but the interior door open. As I walked down the drive, I heard a shriek, and I turned to see Kim bent over the arm of their couch, her robe gone. Pete's pants were down, and he was pumping away at her from behind with his huge cock. Kim looked over her shoulder and locked eyes with me. I took a few steps back toward the door, so I could get a closer look.

"Fuck me! Fuck me!" she shouted, never taking her eyes off me. I stood there, watching them, for I don't know how long—it seemed like forever— when Kim screamed: "I'm cumming, oh my god, you made me cum!" I couldn't tell if she was saying it to Pete or me, but she was still staring directly at me. I heard Pete's familiar grunting, and I knew he was pumping her full of his semen. She continued moaning, her orgasm floating along with Pete's.

I couldn't take any more. I turned on my heel and ran to my car, throwing my bag on the passenger seat and flipping a U-turn to head home. It was twenty-five minutes to my house, but I had to stop after ten, next to an empty field. I laid my seat back and pulled my dress up. I looked down at my pussy as traffic passed me by, and my fingers went to work. I was so insane with desire after *almost* getting head from Kim, then watching Pete fuck her while she talked directly to me the whole time, that I made myself cum in less than a minute. I sat there for a few minutes and kept rubbing my pussy, not wanting the wave to end when my phone buzzed. It was a text from Kim.

That was close. I can't tell if Pete suspected anything. Thanks for being so cool.

"No worries. If he was suspicious, he sure didn't seem to dwell on it. His focus was on other things. ;-)"

The three dots danced forever. I closed my eyes and continued playing with myself while I waited for her reply. The phone buzzed again.

I don't know what it is about you, Darcy. Since you whispered in my ear 27 hours ago, I've masturbated to you 3 times, gone down on my husband, touched and sucked on your tits, came all over your face as you ate me, I fondled and tasted your pussy, and got the fucking of my life from Pete. Even getting fucked by him was hotter with you watching. That's more sexual activity in one day than my body has seen in the last six months, and all I can think about right now is making you cum. It's like you're in my bloodstream now or something, and I can't get enough action! I promise I'll be more daring next time, I won't leave you wanting more.

"Watching you cum with Pete was too much for me. I had to stop on the way home and, um, take care of business."

No kidding? I did that to you*? Again?*

"Yes. I felt like I was going to explode if I didn't satisfy that need. I've never been this crazy for someone."

The three dots did their dance for a few seconds. While Kim was typing, Pete's Range Rover went by, but I don't think he noticed me parked on the side of the road.

I thought Kim was typing something lengthy, but instead, I just got what was becoming our secret code.

Holy shit.

Resistance is Futile
Four Weeks Ago

I worked on a new project all afternoon. One of the European engineers had sent me a page of instructions that were barely in English, and I was having a bitch of a time trying to figure out the details. In an act of mercy, the doorbell rang.

Usually, if I'm not expecting anyone, I don't even get up to answer the door. But I was tired of trying to decipher the engineer's notes, and I needed a break, so I sashayed down the hall and looked through the peephole.

Shit! Pete! What the heck was he doing at my house? We weren't actively fucking any more... although I did leave the invitation open. I opened the door.

"Pete! Come in!" I stepped to the side and waved him in. He walked past me and turned around before I even had a chance to shut the door.

"What are you playing at, Darcy? Are you trying to fuck up my marriage so you can have me to yourself? What's your angle?"

"Whoa, slow down here, Petey. What the hell are you talking about?" I didn't care for the accusation.

"You, doing stuff with my wife, showing up at my house, flashing your pussy at me in front of her. What the fuck was all that?"

My first impulse was to tell him to fuck off, but I could see his point. From his side, worlds were colliding. I took a somewhat softer approach in my response. "Okay, first of all, it's not any of your business who I do stuff with. For your information, your wife asked *me* to go running with her today after she came here and grilled me about *you* yesterday. Secondly, I flashed your wife too, not just you. And, flashing my pussy was an accident, not anything sinister. But don't act like you didn't like seeing it. You were balls deep in Kim twelve seconds later!"

"She grilled you yesterday? When? About what?"

"Late afternoon. About our past, if we'd slept together."

"She must have come over when she went running errands. What did you tell her?"

"The truth. That we dated in college for a few weeks, yes, we used to bang, you broke up with me, and I hadn't seen you for ten years before bumping into you at Krogers."

"And she was okay with that?"

"She seemed fine with it from my side. Did she give you a bunch of shit about it when she got home?"

"Well, no..."

"So, there's your answer. She also told me that she was worried you were cheating on her. So, you were right, she was suspicious. I told her I thought maybe you were just adjusting to life post-baby, and that if she was worried, she could always throw a little sex your way. Maybe it would jump-start her libido too."

"She did come home and suck me off last night," he conceded. "That hasn't happened in several months, and then I felt like I was forcing it on her. Last night she was... hungry for it."

"Well, you're welcome, Pete. One day as her friend, and I have her sucking and fucking you again. What's your problem?"

"It's just, you know... worlds colliding." I almost laughed when he used the exact phrase I thought about moments ago. "I was caught by surprise today. I don't know, I guess my mind was playing tricks on me. I was almost convinced that you were going to do something to break us up. It was driving me crazy all afternoon until I couldn't take it anymore, so I decided to come and confront you. I'm sorry."

Was I trying to break them up? I wondered about that for a second. On a subconscious level, is that what this was about? And if so, which one of them was I trying to steal away from the other? I had a lot of fun fucking Pete, but with Kim, I felt electrified. However, I wasn't interested in marrying either one of them, and I certainly had no desire to be a stepmother. I realized that Pete was saying something. "I'm sorry, Pete, what was that?"

"I said I'm sorry, can you forgive me?"

I gave him a devilish grin. When I got home from Kim's house, I was going to change clothes, but the yellow sundress was comfy, and I just went with it. I still wasn't wearing any underwear. I slid the dress up, showing him my pussy. "Is this what got you so upset today?"

He looked at it, sending a thrill through me. "Darcy..."

"Because you were inside Kim right after you saw it. I feel cheated. I've been horny all afternoon thinking about the two of you fucking right in front of me."

"Wait—what? In front of you?"

"Oh, yeah, I heard her cry out when you put your huge cock in her. I turned around, and I watched you fuck her, Pete. I watched you make her cum, and I know you pumped your load deep inside of her. I was so horny for your cock, I stopped on the way home and made myself cum thinking about it."

I saw his cock move in his pants. It was so easy to manipulate men. He gulped. "I thought I saw your car on the shoulder of the road."

"I saw you drive past. I was finger-fucking myself at that exact moment. If you had stopped, I would have let you put it wherever you wanted." I thought his cock was going to rip his pants open, like a ten-inch version of the Hulk. I touched my slit, using two fingers to spread my lips apart a half inch. Peter's peter flexed in his pants, and he licked his lips. "Come get it, Pete. Give me what I need."

"Darcy, I'm finally getting things back to normal with Kim, I can't do this." He was trying to fight me off, but I knew his little head would win.

"Sure, you can, Pete. You're harder than you've ever been. You want to. Tell me you don't want to fuck me."

"Of course, I want to. I *shouldn't*."

I slid a finger into my pussy. "You mean you're going to leave me unfulfilled twice in one day? After I got Kim revved up for you again? That's not very gentlemanly."

He watched me playing with myself, and I could see his resolve crumbling. I reached out and undid his belt and unbuttoned his pants. He didn't even attempt to stop me. "Oh, Pete, good for you for trying. You're a good man." I pulled his pants down, letting his long, hard cock spring out. "Now, I want to you pretend I'm your wife." I shrugged out of my dress and put four fingers inside myself, getting them good and wet, then wrapped my hand around his cockhead, slickening the sensitive skin with my juices and pulling a hiss from his lips.

I turned and bent over the arm of my couch, my hand still wrapped around him, and guided his cock into my pussy from behind. He moaned and leaned forward, sliding five inches into me, backing out, then slipping in all the way. I lost my balance and fell forward, my face getting buried in a large pillow.

His instincts took command, and Pete drove into me, over and over, forcing my face into the pillow, fucking me so hard I couldn't get upright. I felt him deep, deep inside me, then he'd pull back for what seemed like an age, but still leaving three or four inches inside me, only to drive back in until his balls slapped my clit. Every thrust felt like it was throwing off sparks. My body was a slave to his, but my mind was on someone else.

Kim had worked me up so much earlier in the day I *had to* stop on the way home and play with myself to release the tension, but it was never the same as having someone else release it for you. I imagined what it would be like to finally have Kim's soft, full lips on my pussy, her tongue running over my clit, her fingers inside me. She'd look up at me and see my chest turning red as I climbed the wave, losing myself in the pleasure. I'd look down and see her hungry eyes staring at me, her nose pressed into my clit and her tongue piercing my pussy, and I'd cum, and cum, and cum. "Oh, Kim, fuck me!"

Pete slowed down his rhythm. "What?"

Oh, my god, I'd said that out loud. I made an attempt to cover it. "I said, 'I'm Kim, fuck me!' Don't stop, Pete!"

He renewed his pace, and when I heard him moan and felt the stroke change as his cockhead thickened, I knew he was close. He came inside me, and that first detonation was enough to push me over the edge, and I came too, my pussy clenching and squeezing hard on his exploding cock. He was grunting, pushing into me to the hilt, shooting load after load deep into my pussy. Six, seven times, he pulsed inside me, every time eliciting a tremor of orgasm from me in return.

He leaned over, gasping for air, resting on my back, his cock still inside me. His breath was hot and rapid in my ear. As he spoke, I could feel his aftershocks, and I clenched on him every time he had a tremor. "Darcy, holy shit. Where did all that 'I'm Kim' stuff come from? Jesus Christ, that was hot."

I turned my head sideways. "I wanted you to fuck me like you fucked her today. I want you to come back whenever you want to and do to me what you do to her. If you do her from behind, you'll know you can be doing me from behind later that day. If she rides you, reverse-cowgirl, you'll imagine me doing it too."

"You're the devil, Darcy Ford. God help me, you're the devil, and I can't stay away, no matter how hard I try. You always find a way to make me crave you. To cave into you."

"Mmmm... you wanted to fuck me. That's why you came over. You can admit it."

"Yeah, you're probably right. I think I knew, deep inside, that if you offered it, I would take it."

"I told you, Pete, you can have me whenever you want me. But if you come over here, you'd better be ready to give me the D."

"You're the devil. No question."

I whined as he withdrew from me and pulled his pants up. I lay there, ass in the air, face in the pillow, completely sated for the time being. He stroked my back, making me purr. "I need to get back to work. And forget everything I said before.

You're right, I have no say over who you spend time with. You seem to have a... beneficial effect on Kim. You can hang out with her as much as you want."

That's the plan, I thought. *Not that I needed your permission.*

Best Of Both Worlds

G emma set her glass on the table. "I have a question, and I want an honest answer."

I gulped. With how serious her face was, this couldn't be good. I braced myself. "Have I ever not been honest with you? Fire away."

She gestured at the armrest she was leaning against. "On which end of the couch did this happen? Am I leaning against it right now? Because you could have warned me."

She tried to keep a straight face, but I could see her smirk winning out. "Fuck you, Gemma. You had me scared you were getting all serious on me. And of course, that's the arm I was bent over. You think I want to sit in that spot? There's jizz everywhere."

She laughed that disarming laugh that I loved to hear. "Darcy, I'm starting to think Pete was right. You are the devil!"

"I told you that you would end up not liking me by the time this sordid tale was over. I refilled my glass from the pitcher of margaritas and offered it to Gemma. There was enough left for one more drink.

She waved me off. "No, I have to get home. But before I go, I'm going to say something controversial."

166

I gave her a wary look. "Nothing good ever follows that."

She chuckled. "Well, I know this situation with Kim and Pete isn't going to end well. But did you ever consider that most of your problems stem from a lack of underwear?"

"Hey, isn't that blaming the victim or something?"

"I'm just saying, it seems like every time you take off your underwear, you get into trouble."

"Well, can't you say that about every woman? Or every man, for that matter?"

She laughed again. "Touché! Now that you mention it, I guess most of my relationship troubles started that way too. So, I know something must go horribly wrong, but it seems like you had it all figured out."

"You might think so—in fact, I thought so, too. And for a few glorious days, it really seemed like I had the best of both worlds. But it wasn't long until the wheels came off."

"That will have to be a story for another day. What are you doing tomorrow?"

"It's Saturday, so... nothing. I was maybe going to lay out in the yard and get some sun on this pale Irish skin."

"Come over to my place. Our HOA just remodeled the clubhouse and pool. Better yet, I'll come to get you. Pack your pool gear in a backpack, but dress for a motorcycle ride."

I was puzzled. "Why?"

"Because I'm picking you up on my bike. I'll be here at eight-thirty."

I stared blankly for a minute. We were going for a motorcycle ride? I didn't even know she had a motorcycle.

"I think the phrase you're searching for is 'sounds like a blast, Gemma! See you then.'"

I smiled. "Sorry, I was just thinking about how little I know about you."

"We'll change that. After your story is done, I'll tell you everything you want to know about me."

There was something about this woman that made me want to do whatever she commanded. It bothered me a little—it was a powerless feeling, and I don't like feeling that way, not that I wasn't used to it. It happened more than I cared to admit. And I really loved spending time with her. I still didn't know what direction this relationship was going, but if we just became good friends, I'd be okay with that. "Sounds like a blast, Gemma. See you then."

Gemma got up, unfolding her long, dark legs, and stretched. "Let me help you clean up."

She reminded me of a cat as she moved. Graceful, with purpose, but unassuming. It wasn't an effect she tried for, but every move she made was somehow sexy. "No, you're my guest, you don't clean."

"I'm your *friend*, and friends help clean up."

I knew better than to try to talk her out of it. It took all of ten minutes, and we had all traces of dinner cleaned up, the dishes in the dishwasher, and the pans in the drying rack next to the sink.

I walked her to the door, and she surprised me by turning and giving me a quick kiss on the cheek. "Thanks for the story. I don't want it to end badly, though I know it does. See you in the morning!"

I watched her get into her car and get moving before I shut the door. After I brushed my teeth and hair, I stripped down to my underwear and climbed into bed. As much as I wished things hadn't ended badly, too, I was glad they did. For if they hadn't, I wouldn't have met Gemma, and that would have been a shame. I ran my hands over my bare breasts. Would her hands ever be where mine were? And how did she sleep? Topless, like me, because she hated being restricted by a shirt while she tossed and turned? Or was she a shirt-and-underwear kind of gal? Maybe she wore a teddy. I almost laughed out loud at that one. No one wore a teddy to bed unless they were trying to get laid. And it only stayed on if they were unsuccessful. And—did she think about me while she lay in bed? I smiled at the thought. I hoped so. I'd told her so many of my darkest secrets, she'd have a lot to think about. I drifted off, happily believing that she was in bed at that moment thinking about me—maybe touching herself—and I realized I was really looking forward to the next day.

Get Your Motor Running

I was wearing a pair of jeans over black boots, a white long-sleeved shirt over a sports bra, and had my hair pulled back in a ponytail. I didn't know what kind of motorcycle Gemma had—so I had a denim vest ready in case it was a *bike*—like a Harley; I also had a form-fitting black-and-white leather jacket in case it was more of a crotch rocket. I'd had the leather jacket forever but seldom wore it. I got it when I was going through a bit of a *Kill Bill* phase. Thank god I didn't have the money or the guts to get the yellow outfit Uma wore in that movie.

Gemma, as usual, rolled up a couple of minutes early on a Triumph. I knew nothing about them, but I decided the leather jacket was the better way to go since it more closely matched her outfit.

She wore a pair of jeans that, to my chagrin, looked way better on her than mine did on me, knee-high boots, and a black leather jacket. She took off her flat-black helmet and started up the walk. I shut and locked the door and met her halfway.

"Nice jacket!" she said. "And why do you look so much better in jeans than me? It's not fair."

"I was just thinking the same thing! You wear them way better."

"Well, agree to disagree."

171

We approached the bike, and she handed me a silver helmet she had strapped to the back seat. "It should fit you. It was my first helmet. Are you ready?"

I smiled and pulled the helmet over my head. It was a good fit. "Let's do this!" I shouted.

She pulled away from the curb, rocketing past the twenty-five mile per hour speed limit in what seemed like a half a second. We leaned hard into the curve that merged onto the larger street that exited my neighborhood, past the spot where Kim said she stopped to masturbate after she left my house that first night several weeks ago.

Gemma took us out of the city and up into the mountains, speeding through the curves, slowing down behind tourists who feared driving on the twisting mountain roads. I clung tightly to her, pressing myself against her back and wrapping my arms around her waist. When she leaned, I leaned. When she straightened up, so did I. At this moment, she was very much the alpha.

We were going to head into the national park, but the line stretched more than a half mile into the distance and vanished around a bend. She turned her head and shouted at me. "Good idea, but bad timing! You want to just head back down to my place?"

"Sure!"

She turned us around and headed back down the hill, going through the mountain town that guarded the national park, and down the opposite valley from the one we ascended. If going up was thrilling, going down was fueled by adrenaline. We didn't encounter much traffic because everyone was still heading up for the day, so Gemma let the bike run. I got a peek at the speedometer, and it was just under one hundred twenty miles per hour. My adrenaline spiked, and I felt the quickening when I saw that crazy speed as we leaned hard into each turn, only to straighten the bike and bend the other way for the next curve.

She slowed to a more prudent pace as we edged our way back into town. We wound through the traffic, finally crossing into her neighborhood, and moments later, we pulled into her driveway and rolled to a stop in her garage.

I climbed off the bike and took the helmet off. "That was amazing! It's been a long time since I've been on a motorcycle."

"I'm glad you enjoyed it. I love getting out and just riding. Everything else just fades away. It demands focus, but it feels like flying." She set her helmet on the seat, so I placed mine behind it. She started toward her house but turned and looked back at me. "Are you still down for going to the pool?"

I pointed over my shoulder to my backpack. "I've got all my pool gear. Let's do it!"

"Great! Let's get a quick snack and change, and we'll walk over!"

Inside, we each had Greek yogurt and half an apple, then went to her room to change. While Gemma disappeared into her closet, I sat on the bench at the end of her bed and slipped my boots off, shimmied out of my jeans and let my panties drop to the floor. I slipped on my black string bikini and tied it over my left hip, then wrapped a sheer black sarong around my waist. I took off the white shirt and sports bra, and slipped my top on backward, tied the string, spun the cups around to the front, and got my breasts adjusted in the small triangles of fabric.

I was tying the string around my neck when Gemma came out of the closet in a red bikini with gold chains on each hip holding the skimpy bottoms on, and another one wrapped around her neck to secure the top. "Oh, I love the black on you, Darcy. It looks gorgeous with your burgundy hair."

"Thanks! Red is definitely your color, too."

"You don't think the chains are too much? Too 'look at me'?"

"God, no. It'll be boner town over there when the guys see you."

She cracked up. "That gave me a mental image I'll have a hard time clearing out of my brain. Thanks for that."

I folded my clothes and set them on the bench. Lastly, I slipped my feet into a pair of sandals with a modest one-inch heel. I had a smaller bag in my backpack with my e-reader, phone, Bluetooth headphones, and a little bit of cash in case there was a concession stand at the pool.

Gemma grabbed two bottles of water from the fridge and held one out to me. "You ready?"

I said that I was, and we walked out the front door and headed left at the sidewalk.

"It's just ahead here," Gemma explained. "We go up this path and through a small park, and we're there. It's really something. Since I'm new to the neighborhood, I don't know what it was like before. Apparently, it was run down and closed more than it was open last summer so they could do repairs. I guess they raised the HOA dues to pay for the renovation over the winter and this spring, but everyone seems happy with it."

She was right. As we walked through the park, I could see several different water slides on the other side of a long white fence. She used a keycard to open a gate, and we arrived at her neighborhood's pool. Or two pools. One was massive, had four different water slides dumping into it. It was packed with kids and surrounded by parents yelling at them. Thankfully, we walked right past that one.

The next pool was about three-fourths the size, but with no water slides. It had a diving board on one end where the depth marker read twelve feet. The shallow end was four feet and had a long bench on each side, allowing you to sit and enjoy the water without having to go all the way in. After twenty feet, the seats disappeared, and the floor of the pool dropped away to its ultimate depth.

Several tables with massive umbrellas sticking out from holes in the center were scattered around the perimeter, and dozens of chaise lounges lay everywhere. We grabbed two and pulled them to the area with the best sun, but away from the handful of people who were frolicking in the water.

We put sunscreen on, both of us preferring lotion to the spray-on kind. Gemma handed me her tube. "I hate to be a cliché, but would you do my back? Of course, I'll do you."

Whether she meant it as a double entendre or not, that's how my brain interpreted it. She didn't correct it. She stretched out on her stomach on the chaise while I squirted lotion into my palm. I rubbed it between my hands to warm it up, then started spreading it across her back, rubbing it in circles.

I remembered one of my first trainers talking to me about fitness. "There's a big difference between being skinny and being fit, Darcy," he said. "Both look good, but being fit feels better for you and your partner." I think he assumed I was gay, even though I had only been with one woman—at the frat party—and was dating a man at that time. I didn't correct him, though, because it kept him from hitting on me. But I never forgot what he said, and it's in part why I've spent so much time working out. As I rubbed the lotion into Gemma's dark skin, I could feel her muscles underneath. She wasn't just skinny, she was *fit*. I ran a hand under her strap and an inch or so under the borders of the swatch of fabric that covered half of each of her ass cheeks.

"Mmmmm. I didn't know you would give me a massage. We should have stayed at my place and done it right."

"Oh, I, uh, I'm done," I stammered. I felt myself turn bright red at the realization I'd been doing more than just rubbing lotion on Gemma's back.

She turned her head toward me. "You sure? Because I'll let you do that all afternoon if you want."

"Oh, um... if, you want..." Jesus, once again, I sounded like a teenaged boy falling all over himself for the first girl to let him touch a boob.

"No, it's my turn. Lie down."

I did as she ordered. She started on my shoulders, and I reveled in her touch, even if it was just for the practical application of sunscreen. She spent more time than was necessary and used more pressure than the job called for. She really was giving me a mini massage. Her fingers wandered farther below the edge of my bottoms than they needed to, and I heard a moan escape my throat. I loved every second of it.

"There," she said. "How's that?"

I echoed her earlier phrase. "I'll let you do that all afternoon if you want."

She laughed. "Right? Also, don't look, but when you sit up, the guy at the closest table is trying to use his peripherals to check us out without getting busted by his wife. I bet he's expecting us to make out or something."

"He should be so lucky." *So should I.*

My bag was made for pool-side living, so it came with a cable and combo lock built-in. I tethered it to the chaise, and with our stuff secure, we got in the pool. I could tell Gemma was a much better swimmer than I was, but we weren't in a race. It was a saltwater pool rather than chlorinated, so it was easy on my eyes, and I floated along with ease. We just lazily made our way up and back, then sat on the bench for a few minutes with our elbows up on the deck and our heads laid back, tits thrust toward the sun, absorbing some glorious ultraviolet rays.

"I can feel the vitamin D coursing through my veins," I said absently.

"Oh yeah. And serotonin. There's a reason why the Egyptians worshipped the sun. They just didn't know the science behind it."

After another fifteen minutes, we decided to go back to our chairs. We dipped under and crossed the width of the pool submerged, popping up by the ladder. I'm sure Gemma looked like Phoebe Cates in that scene from *Fast Times at Ridgemont High* as she climbed out of the pool in her red bikini.

The man who had been checking us out earlier was playing a game on a tablet as we passed. He forgot to use his peripherals this time, and I swear he was like that cartoon wolf whose jaw falls to the ground, and his eyes bug out when he sees a woman. His wife, who had her head buried in a book, even noticed us, then saw him staring with his mouth hanging open. I heard her say, "Do you want me to ask if you can take a picture with them, Al?" I stifled a laugh and didn't hear whatever his lame reply was.

We stretched out on the deck chairs, me on my back, and Gemma face down.

"Will you untie my strap?" she asked.

I did so, tossing them to the side so her back wouldn't end up with a tan line. I undid the tie around the back of my neck, letting the strings hang off to the side. I pulled the tops of the fabric triangles down, stopping just shy of my pink nipples, hoping to avoid massive tan lines, though some would be unavoidable. "This is nice," I said as I adjusted my breasts to make sure there were no wardrobe malfunctions. "I needed a day of just doing nothing. Thanks for inviting me over."

"It's my pleasure. I'm glad to have someone to come here with me. It keeps the riff-raff from feeling sorry for the lonely single girl who needs hit upon. I do have a request, though."

"Sure, what is it?"

"Tell me more. We're building to something big. I want more."

I knew that sometime today, we'd get back to this. Gemma really seemed to enjoy relentlessly pulling my past apart. But of course, I would not say no. "Where was I?"

"You had gone down on Kim in the morning and made Pete bang you that afternoon."

"Yes, thanks for putting it so delicately. Do you want to hear this or not?"

"I'm sorry. You made tender, sweet love to Pete that afternoon."

"Fuck off. Okay, so I made Pete bang me like you said, and it seemed I had things all figured out. For a few days, anyway, I was living a double life and loving it."

Chasing Waterfalls
Three Weeks Ago

The next few days were busy with work, and Kim had stuff to do with Becca and some other moms in their neighborhood—birthday parties, playdates, that kind of thing, so we weren't able to hook up again right away.

Pete popped in a couple of times to take me up on my offer. He told me the things he and Kim had been doing to each other, and we reenacted them at my place. He loved it. I think a couple of things he may have made up just to get me to do them because Kim didn't give me those details in her text messages, which she sent every time they did anything sexual.

Four days after I'd gone down on her, Kim texted me.

So... I did a thing.

"Oh, yeah? Do tell."

The three dots bounced around for a minute, and instead of a message, it was a picture of her pussy. She'd gotten a Brazilian wax, leaving a swatch of blonde hair above her labia, which were now as bald as could be.

I couldn't go all the way like yours because I like having a little hair to pull on. But holy hell, is this more comfortable! It makes me feel sexy just walking around. Hurt like hell, though.

"It gets better. The first time is the worst."

That's what the lady told me.

The dots danced again, and another picture came through. This time, it was Kim's pussy with her index and pinky fingers pushing her lips apart, thumb on her clit, and the other two fingers diving inside.

I stared at that image for maybe five seconds before I had my hand in my own pants. What had I awakened in this woman? She was sending me unsolicited vag picks, and I loved it.

While I was staring at her pussy pic, the dots did their dance.

Thinking of you. We'll get together soon. I need to go finish what I just started.

I did too, making myself cum while staring at that gorgeous image.

The next morning, my phone rang, but it was the video call app. I wondered who would be video-calling me, and my heart beat faster when I saw it was Kim.

I answered, even though I was still in bed and topless. I didn't care if she saw my tits; in fact, I wanted her to. I had a flash thought that it might be Pete using her phone, angry because he saw the pussy pics from yesterday. I decided I didn't care if *he* saw my tits, either. I held the phone far enough away that they were in the frame when it connected.

"Hi, Darcy! Sorry, this is so early—oh my, look at that!" She was wearing pajamas. "Um, I wasn't expecting that. Sorry. Damn, you're so hot. Hold on." She set the phone down for a few seconds, and when she came back, she was topless, her bare breasts and perky nipples highlighted in a patch of sun.

"That's much better," I said. "What's up?"

"I was wondering if you wanted to go for a hike tomorrow? I know a great trail, about twelve miles round trip, with a great payoff at the top. I'd want to leave at like six, though, so we can get back in time to pick up Rebecca at daycare."

"Sounds awesome! I've been wondering when we'd get together again."

"I know. I've wanted to so badly. It's tough balancing everything, though."

I slid my panties down with my free hand and hit the reverse button on the camera, the image on the screen flipping from my tits to my other hand as I played with my pussy. I pushed my lips open with a finger, running it north to south, then plunged it inside. "Tell me how badly you've wanted it."

"Oh my god," she moaned. "I wish that was my hand."

"It is. Tell it what to do."

We spent the next ten minutes having phone sex, something I hadn't done since Christmas break my freshman year when my boyfriend went home to Maryland. I racked up a huge phone bill that month, and my dad was pissed.

Kim gave me instructions, and I followed them to the letter. She reversed her camera and stripped off her clothes completely. I saw her put her feet on their kitchen table, and then she focused the camera on her hand, working her pussy in the same way she told me to do. Our hands were in sync, and we both were writhing and moaning. If synchronized masturbation ever becomes an Olympic Sport, we would make the team for sure. Well, maybe we'd be alternates, because she came before I did, screaming, in part because of her orgasm, and in part because she dropped her phone on their tile floor.

It took me a second to get back into the rhythm after she recovered her phone, but she put her camera right on her vagina. I could see the cum glistening on her lips, her swollen clit peeking out from under its hood. She lazily ran a finger through her slit, and she talked me back into focus. I came hard, watching a small flood of my juice rush out on my third contraction. It was kind of hot watching myself cum from another viewpoint, and my orgasm surged and lasted another fifteen seconds.

When I was done, I was out of breath. I hit the reverse button again, flipping the camera back to my face. Kim did the same. She had that lusty look again, just like the other day when she told me to go down on her. "My god, your face is so beautiful after you cum, Darcy. I can't believe I'm going to eat that pussy. I'm ready for you."

My pelvic muscles clenched when she said it. "I can't wait, either. I've been thinking about you all week."

"Six AM tomorrow. Don't be late."

I basked in the afterglow for a few minutes, then got busy getting as much done on my projects as I could so I'd be able to take the impromptu vacation time the next day. I even told Pete I was busy when he texted me, wanting to fuck that afternoon. I wanted to have a clear calendar for Kim.

I rolled to a stop in front of Kim and Pete's house at five 'til six the next morning and got out with my backpack and a big water bottle. The garage door rolled up, and Kim pulled out in an Audi Q5. I'd never seen her car before, not even when she came to my house. With a price tag close to sixty thousand dollars, this was another confirmation that selling insurance paid well.

I climbed in and set my backpack between my feet. Rebecca was in the child seat behind me.

"Hi, Kim! Good morning, Becca!"

"Mos mop," the toddler replied.

Kim reached over and put her hand on my leg, rubbing it from knee to hip a couple times. "I feel like it's been forever since I've seen you. I just need to get Becca to Karen's place, and we're off!"

Sticking to the streets, it took us almost as long to get there as it did when we went running the previous week. I walked in with Kim and Rebecca.

Karen smiled at us when she saw us approach. "Hi, Kim, hi, Darcy! Are you two off on another run?"

I shook my head while Kim ushered Rebecca to the main room. "No, she's taking me on a hike today. Twelve miles, she said, with a great payoff at the top."

"Oh, that sounds nice." She pointed at my vagina, and at Kim's ass. "Do you shop at the same place?"

Confused, I looked down, then at Kim. It took a second, but then it hit me. We were wearing the same brand of Lycra shorts. The only difference was the piping on mine was orange while hers was green. "Oh, wow, I hadn't noticed that. Yeah, I guess we do. You're quite observant, Karen."

Kim returned to us. "Hey, guys. Thanks again, Karen. Becca loves her daycare days. She got so excited when I told her she was coming here today."

"I'm glad. You two have fun on your hike!"

We hopped back in the Audi, and Kim steered us into the mountains on a trip that took an hour through the winding roads. We went all the way to the Elk Basin Ranger Station, and the entry to the national park. She flashed a season pass card, and the ranger at the gate waved us through. After another ten minutes on a rutted single-track dirt road, we arrived at the Whispering Falls and Horseshoe Lake trailhead. While she gathered her things from the back of the Audi, I studied the sign. Whispering Falls – six miles. Horseshoe Lake – seven point five miles.

"You ready?" she asked.

I pulled the pack over my shoulders. "Lead on!"

We walked at a brisk pace for the first couple of miles, but the incline and the altitude were getting to both of us, so we slowed down after that. It was almost ten-thirty before we got to the falls.

In the mid-morning sun, the falls were gorgeous. Pouring out of the top of a rock face, eight cubic feet per second of water fell sixty-five feet into a pool at the base of the cliff. A fine mist rose in a cloud from the impact point. The sun hit this spray and cast out a rainbow across the front of the pool.

"Wow, this is amazing! I've never been up here before. It's definitely worth the hike."

Kim beamed. "I knew you'd like it. But that's not the best part." She pointed to our right. "That trail goes another half mile or so, and then doubles back to a spot right at the top of the falls." She pointed to the left. "But if we go this way, we can climb directly up there and save twenty minutes of hiking."

"And that's something we want to do?"

She smiled. "Oh, yes. We want to."

"Lead the way!"

She bounced off the trail and into the woods. I followed her, dubious about climbing. I didn't feel like breaking any bones on this hike. But she seemed to know what she was doing, so I followed her.

We were about a quarter of the way around the steep rock face. There was a ledge about four feet up, which Kim used her cheerleader's agility to hop onto. I jumped up, getting my hands on the ledge, and pulled my legs up behind me, grunting as I rose from a squat. She was far more graceful than I at this.

Kim was already walking along the ledge, which rose as it went along. We got to the end, now about fifteen feet from the forest floor, and found another shelf, this one a little wider, about two feet above the one on which we stood. Looking up, I could see there were several of these small steps, then the rock face sloped away from view. We climbed to the last level, then Kim nimbly started up the remaining slope. She made it look easy, so I followed. Halfway up, my feet slipped, and I fell flat on my stomach. I started to slide backward and had visions of lying at the base of the cliff, battered and broken.

Kim was there, reaching out and grabbing my hand. I got my feet back under me and scurried to the top.

I looked around. We were at the end of a broad meadow, through the middle of which cut the stream that fed the waterfall. Directly ahead, the trail emerged from the woods, drew close to the stream, and then veered away to the west toward the origin of the water flow.

Kim pointed in the direction where both the stream and the trail disappeared at a point where the pine trees reclaimed the land from the meadow. "If you go another mile that way, you get to Horseshoe Lake. Come over here."

She led me to a hollowed-out depression the size of a large hot tub. It was ringed at the front by tall rocks that stood like teeth. The stream filled the small pool, then the excess water passed between the teeth, creating the waterfall we were looking up at ten minutes earlier.

I was admiring the view when I realized that Kim was sitting on a large rock. She pulled her shoes and socks off, then her shorts and underwear, and finally her shirt and sports bra. Without saying anything, she jumped in the pool.

"Oh, my sweet Jesus, it's cold!" she shouted. Her skin was all goosebumps, her nipples like rocks. "Don't just stand there, get in!"

I was quite surprised by this turn of events, but I rolled with it. I was naked in a minute and hopped in next to Kim. The temperature took my breath from me. It wasn't ice cold, but even in the summer heat, it couldn't have been more than seventy degrees, and that was being generous.

Kim grabbed me and kissed me, her tongue hungry and searching. She put her hands on my shoulders, and I wrapped my arms around her, pulling her close, letting my hands wander over her back and ass.

Her hands found my breasts and my cold-forged nipples, tugging and twisting them playfully. I felt, rather than heard, a gasp escape my mouth. One of my hands drifted toward her stomach, seeking the treasure that resided below, and she grabbed my arm.

"No, not today. Today is about you." She pushed me gently backward until I bumped into a rock outcropping. Its edges were worn smooth by eons of water flowing over it during thousands, or tens of thousands, of spring runoffs. As the summers wore on and the water level dropped, the surface of this rock became exposed, as it was now.

Kim squatted down and wrapped her arms around my legs, just under my ass cheeks. Her face was submerged, and then she lifted me onto the rock. It formed a surprisingly comfortable seat. Once my back adjusted to the cold stone behind me, I leaned back. The outcrop of rock was just enough for my butt to settle onto.

Kim leaned forward, forcing my legs open. I looked down, and my pussy was right at the edge of the stone seat. That was convenient. She began kissing my inner thighs; first, the left, then the right, working her way from the knee to just shy of my excited labia.

"Are you sure you're ready to do this?" I hissed.

"I've been dreaming about it for a week, Darcy. Just please tell me if I'm doing it wrong."

"I'll tell you what the woman who took my pussy-eating virginity told me. Use the bottom of your tongue at first. However much pressure you can apply that way is what you want to use all the time."

"Okay, good tip." Her hands reached up and started roaming around my chest, squeezing my tits, pinching nipples, and tracing circles around my stomach.

When her tongue touched my pussy lips, I felt the quickening. The temperature felt like it went up ten degrees, and I wasn't cold anymore. My hips rocked of their own accord, my pussy trying to reach out to her and take her tongue inside me. Her fingers opened my lips, and then her tongue and one or two—or three, hell, I don't know for sure—fingers were inside me, sliding easily on the slick juice that was flooding out of me. My head rolled back, and I moaned.

I was naked, sitting on a rock, right next to a public hiking trail, at the end of a gorgeous meadow. A naked blonde woman was waist-deep in a pool fed by a fresh mountain stream with her mouth on my pussy. Behind us, water spilled through a rock face and fell sixty-five feet, creating a constant splashing sound. Even in that frat house basement, with a dozen pairs of eyes watching my every move, I didn't feel this exposed, this excited. There was nothing between my naked body and God but a sea of bright-blue sky.

Kim slid her tongue up to my clit, dancing circles around the little hard button of flesh. There are supposedly eight thousand nerve endings in that pea-sized pleasure center, and her tongue hit every one of them. I was riding the wave, climbing to the top of it, coasting along its ridge.

I opened my eyes and looked down, and it was just as I imagined it when Pete had me bent over my couch. Her face was buried in my pussy, her nose just above my clit, her fingers working in and out of me. She looked up and caught me staring at her. I felt her smile, her cheeks rising and pressing against my lips, and she slipped a wet finger into my asshole.

The wave crashed over me. I contracted so hard I pushed Kim's fingers out of me, and a second clench squirted my cum all over her face. I squirted again as she forced her fingers back into me and attacked my pussy like a hungry animal. I kept cumming, over and over, buried by the wave. It was thirty seconds before I realized I was screaming with every contraction. My hips had almost worked their way off the rock, and Kim pushed me back in place, I swear, with her face. I pulled my knees up and lifted my feet close to my head, opening myself to her as much as I possibly could, giving her every bit of my body to play with.

After an eternity lost in orgasm, I finally started to come down. Kim smiled up at me, pleased with herself.

My legs were weak, and every muscle from my abdomen to my anus was tired. I rubbed her silky blonde hair. "Holy shit."

"Fuck yes, holy shit!" She stood upright and gestured to her face and chest, her milky white skin glistening wet in the midday sun. "This is all you. You came all over me. I think you came as much as Pete does. Holy fuck, Darcy, I think I came too. It's hard to tell with my pussy frozen by this water."

As I gradually came to my senses, I saw a figure to my right. A man was approaching from the trail. "Um, Kim..."

"Fuck it. He's already seen us."

I looked at her in awe. "Who *are* you?"

"I'm the woman who just made you cum my first time out of the gate."

The man approached the pool, smiling a broad smile. He was probably mid-forties, in decent shape from what I could see, and his cock was pitching a tent in his hiking shorts. "Hello, ladies. It sounds like you're having quite the time up here."

195

Kim stood to her full five-foot-four and thrust her tits at him. "What of it?" She reached back and put a hand on my pussy. I involuntarily opened my legs for her. I was a rag doll for her to play with. "This is *my* pussy. You can't have it."

He laughed. "As much as I'd love to join you, I just wanted to let you know that there's a bunch of people coming up the trail, maybe five minutes behind me. Everyone's wondering what all the screaming is about."

We sprang into action. It was one thing to taunt this guy with our bodies, but a whole group of people was a different matter. Kim climbed out of the tiny pond, and I slid off the rock and immediately fell, going all the way under the cold water. When I resurfaced, Kim was extending her hand to me and helped me crawl out.

We hurriedly threw on our shorts and shirts, stuffing our bras and panties in our backpacks. We tied our shoes, forgoing trying to get dry socks over wet feet. The man stood and watched us the entire time, a look of amusement on his face.

"Thanks for the warning," Kim said, and she headed back the way we came.

"No problem," the man said. "If you want to get in touch, I'm tagged in photos on the Elk Basin Facebook page. I come up here all the time. I'm probably setting myself up for rejection, but hey, it's worth a shot, right? I don't know if I could make you scream like she just did, though."

"No one ever has," I said and hurried after Kim.

She helped me climb down the rock face, and in another ten minutes, we were back on the trail headed to the car. Our wet feet had carried a bunch of debris into our shoes, so we stopped to clean them out and put our socks on to avoid getting blisters. There were too many people on the trail for us to risk stripping to put on our underwear, so we just went commando the rest of the hike down.

Kim looked over at me every now and then, and I couldn't help but grin from ear to ear. My dad would have called it a "shit-eating grin." I don't know what that means, exactly, or why eating shit would make you grin, but I had one plastered across my face. Finally, she said, "What!?"

I raised my voice to imitate hers. "This pussy is mine. You can't have it."

She blushed. "I was caught in the moment. Oh, god, it was so thrilling to be naked up there, standing in front of that guy with your cum all over me. I feel so *dirty*, but so *awesome* at the same time. That probably doesn't make any sense to you."

I thought about the frat house a decade earlier. "I know the feeling. Equal parts shame and empowerment."

"I'm not ashamed, though. At all. I ate pussy today and made you cum like, like, I don't know what. You *squirted* me. I will remember this day for the rest of my life."

"That's only the second time that's happened. How did you know about that spot?"

She blushed again. "I gave a guy head there in high school."

"Oh, my god! You have a favorite spot! I bet you take all the girls there."

"You didn't seem to mind."

"Fuck, no. I gave you everything I had today. That was incredible. *You* were incredible."

She smiled, beaming with pride, and reached over and took my hand, giving it a squeeze, and laced her fingers through mine. "Now we're even."

Busted Again
Three Weeks Ago

We got back to the daycare center at three-thirty. While Kim went to collect Becca, Karen called me over to the front desk. She had a stern look that made me feel like I was being called to the principal's office. She glanced around, making sure no one else was within earshot. "I don't know what's happening between the two of you, but you need to be more careful."

My first thought was, "How did she know?" but she answered that for me.

"You left wearing a bra and shorts with orange piping. You return with no bra and wearing Kim's shorts with green piping."

I was caught completely flat-footed. "I don't know what to say. I—"

"You clearly had taken your clothes off and got dressed in such a hurry you weren't paying attention to what went with whom. Now, why would you two be naked in the mountains with your clothes in a heap together? Come on, Darcy, it doesn't take a genius to figure this one out. I've seen how you look at each other."

"Karen, I—*we*—would appreciate your discretion. We're just... having fun."

199

"Oh, I'm not going to say anything to anyone. It's not my place, and I'll be the last person to judge. But you can't be this careless and keep it a secret. The women in this neighborhood love to talk. Some of them are quite... uptight in their views about sexuality and would not care for this kind of behavior. I'm not one of those women, but I worry about Kim's family life, her relationship with her husband. I hope you two know what you're doing." She wrote something on a business card and slid it to me. "I'd appreciate your discretion as well."

She walked off to tend to something else. I flipped the card over.

758-5487. No strings. No commitment.

I looked from the card to Karen. She gave me a wink, her stony façade cracking for just a moment. I was puzzling over this development when Kim returned with Becca. Karen, for her part, acted like she knew nothing, fussing over Becca and telling Kim how much of a joy her daughter was.

In the car, I pointed to my shorts. *Kim's* shorts. I didn't tell her that Karen had spotted the switch. "In all the excitement, I didn't notice that we swapped shorts."

She smiled. "We can swap them back at my house. I noticed the switch when we were on the trail, but I didn't say anything. I liked having my pussy where yours had been. It was vaguely... thrilling. Is that weird?"

I thought about the plaid G-string in my underwear drawer at home. "No, not so much."

We came around the curve and saw Pete's Range Rover in their driveway. "Oh, Pete's home early. I guess we'll have to swap shorts later."

I felt a little let down. I wanted to play with Kim a little more before I left, but it was not to be. "No worries. I'll bring them back next time I come over."

Little did I know the next time I came over would also be the last.

Let's Be Naughty

Gemma and I had both flipped twice by the time I finished my story, and we figured we'd absorbed enough ultraviolet radiation for the day. We re-tied our bikinis and got in the pool, swimming a couple of lengths, drifting along, just enjoying the water for a few minutes more. After we climbed out, we gathered our gear and started the walk back to Gemma's house. She didn't put on her sarong, so neither did I. It felt a little risqué parading through the park in just our bikinis—but I must admit, I liked the whistles we got from the guys playing soccer. A couple of them were pretty cute, too, but I much preferred watching Gemma's hips sway back and forth as she walked to looking at the men. She was bringing out the hunger I wasn't sure would ever come back. I just didn't know if she felt the same way.

Back at Gemma's, we went to her bedroom to change. Since the pool was saltwater and not chlorinated, we opted to skip showers and just put on more comfortable clothes. Gemma stood topless in front of her mirror for a moment. "Oh, man, I have tan lines now. Looks like I'll be naked in the backyard for the next few times I lay out."

I looked over. It was the first time I'd seen Gemma without clothes. Well, without a top, anyway. Her breasts were about the same size as mine, like everything else about her, but her nipples were darker, more of a brown than the pinkish color of mine; her skin tone belied her Italian heritage, while mine was due to my Irish roots. Hers shrank down to a smaller size than mine when they got hard, too—which they were right now. It was like the difference between a quarter and a fifty-cent piece. She saw me staring at her and smiled but didn't say anything. She dropped her bottoms to the floor and looked at the reflection of her pubic area. So did I.

She was waxed clean like me. I felt a quickening run through me as she ran her fingers along her hip joints, where the swatch of bikini fabric had covered her pussy. "Yep. Definitely going to have to get rid of these tan lines. I wish we could layout naked at that pool. Can you imagine the whiplash guys like that one today would get?"

My throat dried up when I tried to respond, so I coughed once. "For—ahem—sure. Al's wife would kill him."

"Or kill us. Oh, well." She bent down, retrieved her suit, and disappeared into the closet. I took my suit off and was putting on fresh underwear when she startled me. "Wow, you really got some tan lines today, too." I felt myself stiffen as she touched my left butt cheek, running it along the line left by my suit. Her fingers on my bare ass sent shivers through me and raised goosebumps all over my body. She had to see the effect her touch had. I was getting wet, and my heart began to race. "Your complexion tans quicker than mine. You're going to have a hard time getting rid of those lines. If that's something you want to do, that is. They're kinda sexy."

"I, uh, usually just go to a tanning bed a few times, and it evens out."

"Me too, but I like laying in my yard naked. It feels decadent. Hey, Darcy—let's be naughty!"

Was this it? Was she going to make a move? I felt another surge run through me. I was already wet from her touching me a moment ago. I knew that I wanted this to happen. I always knew that, but I was gun-shy, and her mixed signals forced me to be aloof. Though, to be fair, her messages were getting less confused as time went on. I just didn't want to make the wrong assumption and ruin the friendship. "What did you have in mind?" I turned, with only one leg in my underwear, exposing my pussy to her for the first time.

She was wearing cotton shorts and a string tank top with no bra. She stole a look at my crotch before answering. "Let's order pizza!"

She had to be fucking with me. She had to know her show in front of the mirror, and all her talk of being naked would get my motor running, and her light touch on my bare ass would have me primed. I felt like an idiot with my beaver hanging out in the breeze, so I slipped my other leg through the high-rise panties, covered with hearts like all my underwear were, and pulled them up. Hopefully, I hid my disappointment. "Pizza actually sounds great. I like pepperoni."

"Me too! How are you with pepperoncini?"

"Love them."

"Perfect. I'll order and pour some wine, and you come out when you're dressed."

She bounced out of the room. I thought for a nanosecond about masturbating to take care of the electricity I had running through me, but it wasn't the right time. Or place, for that matter. I slipped my jeans on, harnessed my breasts behind a strapless bra, put on a string tank like Gemma's, and went to join her on the couch. I had just one more story to tell, and she'd be all caught up on my tale of woe. I knew she'd want to hear it after dinner, and I wanted to be done with it after tonight, anyway.

I met her in the living room as she was pouring the wine. "Pizza will be here in forty minutes. I have some cheese and crackers for a snack."

"Well, get them out, so I'm not drinking on an empty stomach. The last part of this ghastly tale will require an iron constitution to get through."

She smiled as she pulled a prepared cheese tray from the fridge. "I was hoping you'd tell me the rest tonight!"

I sipped the wine and munched on a piece of cheese. "Well, strap in, Gemma. This part gets bumpy."

A Star Is Born. Again.
Two and a half weeks ago

I t was odd... I didn't get a call or text from Kim for a couple of days. She usually was buzzing in my phone a few times a day. I texted her a few times but got no response. Pete didn't visit me either. I assumed they were just busy with their kid's activities, or maybe they were enjoying each other now that their sex life was reanimated, but something was nagging at me.

Perhaps she was feeling guilty about going down on me. She did have some hang-ups about same-sex activities. Could she have developed cold feet? I hoped not, because together, we were electric, and it's not like I was asking her to move in with me and swear off dicks for the rest of her life. I was more than happy with having the occasional romp with her; of course, it helped to have her husband's P in my V every few days too. Best of both worlds—except right now, I had neither one.

Finally, on Friday afternoon, I got a text from Kim.

Can you come over tonight? I need you.

I felt relief wash over me. Maybe things were going to be okay! I typed my reply. "Sure! What time? What can I bring?"

The three dots did their dance.

Five-thirty? And just bring you. Clothing optional. ;-)

Five-thirty gave me a couple of hours to wrap up work, shower, make myself as fuckable as possible, and get over to her place. I moved like a hummingbird to get everything done.

I arrived at her place at five twenty-five wearing a pair of tight shorts—not hot pants, but not cargo-length either—and a ribbed sleeveless top that left about three inches of my stomach exposed. I was going for a fuckable look, but not so over the top that Pete would get suspicious if he came home while I was still there. Underneath I had on white lace panties, with embroidered hearts, and a lace bra. I was a package waiting to be unwrapped.

I rang the bell. The inner door was open a few inches, and I heard Kim say, "Come in." I pulled the screen door open and pushed the inner door wider. The living room was dim, and Kim sat on the far side in a leather chair.

Naked.

I shut the door and stalked toward her. "You're no fun. I was looking forward to undressing you."

Her face was deadly serious. She pointed a finger at me and commanded, "Strip."

I gave her a funny look. What was going on? Were we doing some role play I wasn't aware of?

She kept her mug looking mean. "Strip," she said again, "Or leave."

"Okay..." I kicked off my shoes and shimmied out of my shorts. She stared at my underwear while I slipped my shirt off.

"All the way."

I reached behind my back and unhooked the bra and let it fall to the floor. Kim remained stone-faced while I hooked my thumbs in the waistband of my underwear, slid them over my hips and let them drop gently to the carpet. I felt a little funny, standing before her, naked and hairless and unsure what she was playing at. But I wanted her, so I played along.

She pointed at the carpet in front of her. "Kneel."

I knelt down in front of the chair, and she slid her hips forward. I didn't need instructions for that move. I guess she wanted to get right to it. I leaned in and kissed her knees. She lifted her legs and spread them wide, giving me full access to her goods. It was like a treasure chest topped with her closely trimmed golden hair. I kept kissing her legs, moving my way up her thighs toward her waiting pussy.

"Let me tell you a story," she said. I looked up at her. "Don't stop, keep going, and listen."

I didn't especially like this bossy persona she was putting on, but I wanted her to cum, and maybe she'd return the favor afterward. I neared her delicious-smelling blonde beaver.

"After our trip to the mountains the other day, I was gathering clothes to do laundry. Pete grabbed my bag and emptied it, throwing my sports bra and panties at me. *Your* panties, covered in hearts."

I looked up at her, and she pushed my head back down. I licked the crease where her thigh ended, and her groin began. She writhed and moaned a little as I moved from that sensitive area to the more sensitive one dead center.

"Mmmm. Anyway, I picked up *your* panties, realizing that in our rush to get away from the pond in the mountains, I had grabbed *your* underwear and stuffed them in *my* bag. Totally my fault."

I stopped licking her slit to say "no problem," but she pushed my face into her pussy again.

"But what happened next, Darcy, is *your* fault."

I froze for a minute. This didn't sound good.

"Pete looked at me, holding that heart-covered underwear, and the sweet, dumb guy blurted out, *'Hey, those look just like Darcy's.'*"

Alarm bells sounded in my head. *Oh, shit. Pete, you idiot!*

"You can imagine the questions that went through my head, can't you? But I knew the answers to all of them the second he said it. You've been fucking my husband, Darcy. Of course, Pete's not a complete fool. He knew the only way I'd have your underwear is if you'd taken them off around me, and the only reason that would happen is if *we were fucking too.*"

My tongue stopped mid-lick. I looked up at her. "Kim—"

"Keep licking my pussy, Darcy. It's the least you can do after you lied to both of us."

My mind was swirling. What the fuck was going on?

I should just get up and leave. This has gotten too weird.

As I had that thought, something touched me from behind, and I jumped, whipping my head around to see what it was. It was Pete, naked and erect. He laid a hand on my ass and traced a path down my crack and between my legs. I was really confused now, but I spread my legs a little to give his hand room to move.

Kim grabbed my head and pulled it toward her. "Eyes front, Darcy."

I looked her in the eye. Her face was still an emotionless mask.

"So, Pete and I compared notes, and we decided that we couldn't be angry at each other for giving into your wiles. You're very intoxicating. If you could, in less than twenty-four hours, talk me into lesbian sex for the first time, I can certainly understand why Pete couldn't resist you."

Despite the weird tension of the moment, my pussy was getting wet from Pete's persistent fingers stroking it. He leaned forward, sliding his fingers into me. He withdrew them, and his hard cock slid over my pussy and poked my stomach while he reached around and grabbed my breasts as they hung loose underneath me. I heard a moan escape my mouth, very much against my will.

"That's it, Darcy, get into it." Kim was still bossy. "Eat me like you did last week. Show me that passion you used to seduce me."

I resumed splitting her lips with my tongue, running it from south to north, and I slid two fingers in behind it. Despite her stone-faced demeanor, she was wet and ready for me. If she were intent on playing this game, I'd play along.

"Ooh, that's more like it. As I said, I could totally understand why Pete would fall for you, especially the line he told me you used about how his number wouldn't go up since you'd already had him inside you from before. Oh, yeah, faster with those fingers. Fuck, that feels good. But Pete was shocked at how easy it was for you to get me to switch sides, even if it was just for the sheer thrill of it. I guess—oh shit, that tongue is everywhere—I was never as prim and proper as I thought I was. But the funny thing is, Pete was turned on by it. He attacked me and fucked me like he never had before, and I let him do everything to me, Darcy. *Every*thing. It was like Caligula in our bedroom that night. So, we decided we needed to get the three of us together. Oh! Shit, don't you dare stop that, Darcy! Oh, fuck, this is hot. Fuck her, Pete."

Pete sat upright again and started rubbing his cock against my slit. I lowered my back, tilting my pelvis up and giving him a better angle to enter me. I still wasn't sure what the endgame was here, but Kim's hips were bucking, and I wanted that cock inside me, so I went for it on both ends.

He slid into me, driving to the base in one shot. It hurt a little, but when he backed out and thrust in again, his ten-inch rod was slippery from my juices. He pounded me, hard, driving my face into Kim's crotch.

Kim reacted like I'd hit her with an electric shock. "Fuck! Yes, Pete, pound her cunt hard! Fuck me with her face!"

Pete increased his speed, ramming me with every inch he had, bottoming out so hard his balls swung forward and banged against my clit. Every time his sack hit me, it felt like the bumpers on a pinball table lighting up. I let his momentum drive my face into Kim's pussy, letting my tongue ram her clit. I kept my arm locked in place, so my fingers drove in and out of her in the same rhythm as Pete's pounding.

She was as wet as I'd seen her. Her juices were spraying around my fingers with each thrust. My hand was soaked, so I readied two fingers, and on the next push, I deployed them to her asshole. I was doing the Vulcan salute into her holes, two fingers in each. Instead of the Shocker, this was the Spocker.

Kim loved it. "Oh, my fuck! Pete, keep using her to fuck me! She's in my pussy and my ass! Oh, shit, fuck me, fuck me!"

Pete was getting worked into a frenzy. Apparently, I was extra juicy as well, because I felt a wet hand slap me on the backside, and Pete pushed a thumb into *my* ass.

I lost focus for a minute. I was trying to bring Kim's orgasm to a boil, but mine was about to explode. I felt Pete's stroke change as his cockhead swelled, and that did it. I screamed into Kim's pussy as I came in a gushing, violent explosion that would have shoved a lesser cock out of me. But not Pete's long rod.

Pete came in a fury, thrust after thrust sending his massive load deep into me, one pulse at a time. It sounded like a waterbed had sprung a leak, there was so much fluid going in and out of my pussy.

Kim wrapped her legs around my head, grinding her hips into my face, squirting her cum with a force almost equal to her husband's. One squirt blasted my face and ricocheted up and over my head, splattering on my back.

The three of us rocked and convulsed in a triple orgasm that seemed to last forever. Kim's screams blended with mine, and mine with Pete's. It was the greatest sexual experience of my life, pushing the mountaintop to second place, and that night long ago in the frat house down to third. Maybe it was because of the deeper connections I felt with these two. Maybe things were going to be okay between us.

H.A. Blackwood

Pete withdrew both his cock and his thumb, and Kim pushed me away with her feet. My weak limbs gave out, and I collapsed in a heap on the floor, used up, drenched and covered in their cum, and loving it.

I sighed and rolled onto my back, blissfully smiling, and opened my eyes.

What the fuck?

I sat up, staring at the back of Pete's phone. "Were you filming this?" He didn't say anything. I saw Kim walking behind him with something in her arms. Fuck! My clothes! "Kim! What the hell are you doing?"

She didn't respond. Instead, she walked to the front door, opened it, pushed the screen door open, and threw my clothes and my small purse out into their front yard. My mouth hung open for a second as I felt anger replacing the bliss inside me. "Kim? What the fuck is that about?"

"It's about you getting out of my house, you lying, manipulative whore."

"What? I—I don't—"

She mocked me. "I—I—I don't care, Darcy. You lied to Pete, and you lied to me, all for your own selfish reasons. I trusted you, I confided in you, and the whole time you were fucking my husband behind my back. You didn't even have the decency to end it

216

after you started fucking *me!* You were using us for sex, so we just used you. This was great—I mean *holy shit,* right?—but it's over. Thanks for the memories, now get. Out. Of. My. House."

I walked to the door, turning at the last second. "Kim, Pete—"

Pete spoke this time. "Darce, just go. Don't make this harder than it has to be."

I walked outside, naked, with Pete's semen running down my legs. I think they expected me to scurry and collect my things, but I wouldn't give them the satisfaction. I calmly picked up my clothes, one piece at a time. I checked my little bag to make sure everything was still inside.

I glanced back at the house, and in the shadows of the doorway, I could see Pete, still filming. I flipped him the bird and strode to my car with my head held up high. A car drove past, slowing down when the driver caught sight of me. I smiled and waved, laughing as they pulled into the neighboring driveway. Pete and Kim would have some explaining to do with the neighbors. I remembered Karen saying the neighborhood women wouldn't dig this kind of behavior. I smiled, hoping it would cause them a lot of problems. Maybe they'd have to move.

I tossed my things in the car and got in, still naked. I backed out of the driveway and sped off toward home.

I hadn't even made it a block before I started to tremble, my adrenaline ebbing, and I pulled over. The second the transmission clicked into "park," I started crying. I pounded the steering wheel, furious at the situation. Furious at myself for not getting up and leaving when I had the fleeting thought to do so. Furious at Kim and Pete for giving me such a beautiful, soul-cleansing orgasm, and then stomping it to death.

I got my sobs under control and was preparing to pull back onto the road when my phone buzzed. It was Pete.

I opened the text app, part of me hoping it would say, *"We're sorry, come back, stay the night."* I sniffed back at the snot that my tears had worked up and laughed at myself. *Don't be naïve, dummy.*

The text was just a URL for a website. A porn website. My blood ran cold. I clicked it.

The browser opened and spun for a minute, then started a video with the title *Couple Takes Revenge on Dumb, Lying, Whore.*

It started with Pete walking in behind me. He aimed the lens low enough that you couldn't see Kim's face, but you could hear her telling me to strip, which I did, and telling me to kneel, which I also did. I started eating her out while she narrated her story of Pete finding my underwear. I scrolled ahead, watching my head bouncing on Kim's pussy at a comical speed, then seeing Pete slam in and out of me fast enough to start a fire. When Kim kicked me to the floor, I stopped scrolling and let it play through. It ended with me in the yard, naked, picking up my stuff, and flipping the camera the bird.

I sighed and sniffed back more snot. What I thought was indignant pride in the way I gathered my stuff on their lawn looked pathetic on video. I looked like a hooker, like someone who would lie and cheat on spouses and walk around naked in public. In fact, that's exactly what I was. I started crying again, this time not from anger, but out of shame. I looked at my phone again. The video already had thirty views and a ninety-five percent rating. People loved my humiliation. Fuck me.

I put the car in drive and made it home without having another meltdown. I pulled into the garage and walked to the house, still naked. I didn't care if the neighbors saw me. *This is who I am. The naked whoring whore.*

Inside, I went straight to the shower and washed the night off me. I checked my phone to see if there were any more messages. There were none.

I crawled into bed and watched the video again, this time not scrolling through it. It was twenty minutes long, and I watched every second of it. It was over one hundred fifty views and still rated ninety-four percent. I scrolled down, and the recommended videos were all some form of revenge porn. Nothing rated above eighty-two percent.

You are NOT proud of your rating!

There were comments now, too. Of course, I read them, poor grammar and all. I had to rub my own nose in the degradation.

"She hot as shit! Damn, I need me a bitch like that."

"Fucking LOL. Shame! Shame! Shame!"

"How do they figure they got revenge? She fucked them both separate, then fucked them together, then left like she don't give two shits. Seems like she got hers and bounced. Those fools got played."

"Shit, that looked real. I know it ain't, tho, it's scripted, but damn that girl can act."

"Did you see that dude's hog? Long as fuck but skinny. I like them thick, I want my pussy filled the fuck up."

That one had a reply: "*Dis bitch loved that skinny wang fo sho, and she took it all.*"

I chuckled at that one. Fo' sho'. There were more.

"*Only a white boy would have a cunt wrench that long and have no meat on it. What a waste of inches. Bitch, you read this, HMU. I got what U need.*"

I laughed out loud this time. *Cunt wrench?* I'd use that one in the future, I was sure.

While I didn't care for being referred to as "bitch" so much, I felt better knowing that none of these perverts were judging me, and they were making fun of Pete as much as me in any case. I smiled, set my phone on the charger, and drifted off to sleep.

Heart Returned

Gemma finished the last slice of the pizza and tossed the crust in the box with the other seven.

"Ah, nothing left but the bones," she said. "I haven't had pizza in forever. God, that was good."

I leaned back on the couch, hands on my gut. I swear I could feel every bit of those four slices pushing my stomach out, but Gemma was right. Pizza was a rare treat, and the local place she ordered from was way better than the chain stores.

She picked up her phone and started messing with it. I was getting a little nervous—she hadn't had much reaction to my story other than, "I can't fucking believe they did that to you." Suddenly she exclaimed, "Holy shit!"

"What?" I asked. Were my exploits finally too much for her?

"Your video has *one hundred thousand views!* And it's still rated ninety-three percent!"

"You found it? Oh, man. Please, forget you saw it."

She smiled at me with that Gemma smile. "Forget I know a legit porn star? You know, I don't think a hundred thousand people saw the last Travolta film."

"You know I'm not proud of it, right?"

"I know. I wonder if Pete and Kim are making money from it. You could sue them for royalties."

I sighed. "I don't want to talk about that anymore. I don't want to talk *to them* anymore, especially not about this video."

"Okay."

We settled into an awkward silence, which was rare for the two of us. I stared at her for a minute, until she looked up at me and we locked eyes. I smiled. "Ninety-three percent, huh?"

That was the perfect tension breaker. Gemma laughed like I'd caught her off guard with my comment. The sound of her laughter warmed me inside. She looked toward the kitchen. "You want something to drink?"

I paused for a second. Gemma drove me here on her motorcycle, so I'd need a ride home. "Yes, I do. I can call an Uber when I'm ready to go."

"Or you could just stay here tonight. This couch is really comfy, especially if you're drunk."

Another mixed signal. An invite to stay, but not in the same room. But, after reliving the night that was both the best and most awful of my life, I decided I could use a night of drinks where one of us didn't have to leave at the end of it.

I nodded. "Okay, that sounds good. Let's drink."

I started to get up to help. Gemma smiled as she gathered ingredients. "No, you stay there. I'll be right back."

I lay back on the couch and closed my eyes for a couple of minutes, visions of my humiliation swimming through my head. Where was this thing with Gemma going? It was like she was taking me through an extended therapy session, making me relieve my past and come to terms with it. But come to terms with what? Why was I so hard on myself? I liked sex. I wanted sex with men and with women. I enjoyed both equally, but they satisfied me in different ways. I wasn't ashamed of that. And why should I be ashamed of that video? We have celebrities today who we only know because of a sex tape.

"Hey, wake up!"

I opened my eyes to find Gemma holding a glass out to me. I sat up and grabbed it from her. Knowing everything she made was sensational, I took a drink without even knowing what it was. "Wow, this is delicious! Is that mint?"

"Yeah. It's a mojito. Or a reasonable imitation. I thought it sounded good after a day of fun in the sun."

I took a long drink, sucking through the straw like it was my job. Damn, it was good. "I've heard of these, but can you believe I've never had one?"

"I love them, but they sneak up on you." She flashed a wicked grin. "That's why I made a pitcher of them."

"That will suffice, I think." As if she needed to get me drunk to do whatever she wanted to me. Which reminded me, "Oh, Gemma, I forgot. A week after, uh, *that night*, I called Karen."

"The daycare lady?"

"Yes."

"Oh, my god! Did you two fuck?"

"Uh-huh. It was a moment of weakness. I had gone from daily, sometimes twice daily, sex to zero. It was a hard transition, and I was feeling sorry for myself. I think I also wanted an ego boost."

"What was it like?"

"She asked me over to her place. I don't want to get into the details on this one, but let's just say she likes leather and bondage."

"Did you—"

"Yes. Yes, I did. She went easy on me, and she's very... capable. But that patrician, bossy façade carried over to her leather-clad persona. It was fun, don't get me wrong, but not what I was looking for. At least not right now."

"What are you looking for?"

I took another long drink of the mojito, thinking about the way Gemma had turned me on so much in her room earlier, before leaving me standing half naked to go order pizza. Either she was fucking with me, or I was too much of a coward to act when presented with the opportunity. "You mean, what do I want?"

"Yeah, that's what I'm asking you. What do you want?"

"I want to be happy."

"Everyone wants that."

"I want to be happy being myself."

"Again, everyone wants—"

I was done. After everything I'd been through in the last few weeks with Kim and Pete, after a solid week of storytelling, after all the time Gemma and I spent together—and most of the evenings we'd spent together you could make a case were dates—I was done beating around the bush. "I want *you*, alright? I want you. I'm tired of dancing around it. You've been making me tell you all my darkest secrets, parading your *perfect* body in front of me for a week now, sending me mixed signals, and I can't take it anymore. I want *you*."

I took a breath. There. It was out in the open. After tonight there would be no more guessing.

Gemma was either into me or she wasn't. But I wouldn't have to wonder which wat she was leaning for much longer.

She smiled at me. "Finally! I was starting to wonder if you would ever come out and say it!"

"You mean you've been toying with me all this time?"

"No, not at all. I've just been waiting for you to regain your confidence. The same confidence you had when you went up to Kim—in front of her husband, no less—and told her you wanted her. I know those weren't your exact words, but that's what you meant, and that's what she heard. Do you know the size of the fucking lady-balls it took to do that? And you got what you wanted! You had your face buried in a hetero ex-cheerleader's muff in *one day*. And when you wanted Peter's peter, you just brought him back to your place and had your way with him. And you got what you wanted in that frat house years ago. You're a force of nature, Darcy. Whenever you've wanted something, you've just gone and gotten it. I've given you so many openings, waiting for you to reclaim your mojo and make a move, but you weren't ready, and I didn't want to push it on you. I thought clearing out your mental baggage would help you get there." She grinned. "And it worked. See, I'm so smart!"

I wasn't sure what to think. She *had* been walking me through a week of therapy! Maybe it *was* good for me to get it all out in the open like that. And, from my side, at least, there were no secrets. I'd told her everything there was to know about Darcy Ford, and she hadn't run away.

She sipped her mojito. "I have a secret to tell you before we go any farther."

"Well, it's about time you told me something. I've dumped all my dirty laundry on the table. It's your turn."

"It's more of a showing kind of secret."

This was more intriguing. "Okay, show me."

She stood up and untied the strings on her shorts. I felt a flutter inside. What could she show me that I hadn't seen in the mirror in her room?

Gemma hooked her thumbs in the waistband, and her shorts slid down her brown legs, puddling up at her feet. She stood in front of me wearing white, high-cut panties.

With a single red heart in the center.

My mind flashed back to the frat house the morning after my exploits when the woman who first turned me on to the pleasures of the female form had disappeared with my underwear. *This* underwear.

"Look familiar?"

"You've got to be kidding me! It was *you* this whole time?" I was actually kind of angry.

She shrugged. "Looks that way."

"You knew this whole time that you were the one who got away? And you didn't tell me? Why?"

"I knew the minute I saw you in the gym. I've never forgotten you. I was curious to find out what that night meant to you. What I meant to you, if anything. Then when we started going through your past, it never seemed like the right moment to tell you. Plus, I was worried that you would get turned off by the truth about why I was there that night."

"Well, I don't know the truth about why you were there, do I? Why don't you enlighten me and see what happens?"

She sighed. "Okay, here goes. Darcy, I was a stripper when we met. Well, a stripper and more, you might say. The frat guys paid me to come to that party. Like, they spent a *lot*—at least a lot for me back then. When I met you in that basement, at first, it was just part of the job. I was paid to fuck a woman and see where it went from there.

"Yes, I'd been with women before, but it was always part of an act. Gay for pay, that kind of thing. We made buckets of cash at the club with that stuff. But I'd never been with someone who was doing it because she *enjoyed* it. Your orgasm that night wasn't fake, and for the first time, neither was mine. You were one hundred percent into it, and you sparked something in me. Afterward—well, I had to leave. I didn't think you'd like me if you knew who I was. *What* I was.

"So, I left early, but I wanted something to remember you by." She snapped the waistband on the panties. "I've kept these for a decade. Like you, I've worn them a handful of times when I wanted to feel special, but otherwise, they've just stared at me from my top drawer, reminding me of a time when I fell for a girl I was hired to fuck.

"So—this is your chance, Darcy. I understand if you're furious, or hate me for leaving you that morning, or whatever. But before anything happens between us, I had to tell you the truth about who I am. Who I was."

I stared at her for a second. She was scared. This perfect specimen, this *goddess* was frightened that *I* was going to reject *her*. The angry impulse I had at first faded. "I've had this feeling of familiarity from the moment you introduced yourself to me at the gym. I've just felt... at ease with you. Now I know why. I've carried you in my heart for ten years."

"Do you still want me?"

I bit my lip. She wasn't perfect. Like me, she was worried her past would make her unpalatable to someone else. But the reality, the reconciling of who she was with who she is added a dimension to her that only made her more alluring. "More than ever."

"If I'd told you at the beginning, would you want me like you do right now?"

I thought for a second. "Probably not. I know it's only been a little more than a week, but I wasn't ready for you then. Kim's rejection was too fresh, and it would have been too much to process."

She smiled, satisfied she'd made the right call. "Did you really start getting waxed because of me?"

I laughed. "Yes. I never considered it until I went down on you. Bald is beautiful! So, you were really a stripper? Like, at a club?"

"Yep. Do you remember Poppa Chubby's near the interstate?"

"Oh my god, yes! We always used to laugh at that name. You worked there?"

"Six nights a week, off on Sundays, until that night with you."

"You quit after the night at the frat?"

"Yes. I felt like I'd missed an opportunity to be with you because of that job. That's why I left town and went to California. I wanted a fresh start, but Cali wasn't all it was cracked up to be, either."

"It sounds like there are some stories behind that statement."

"They rival yours, Darcy. And I'll tell you all of them. Another time." She set her glass down and held up her phone, taunting me with the sex tape Kim and Pete had posted. "Right now, there's this twenty-minute movie I want to watch with you."

I reached for her phone, trying to snatch it from her hand. "No! Give it here!"

She was too fast for me and scurried down the hall toward her room. I got up in a flash and went after her. Her tank top lay in the hallway. I shed mine and reached back to unhook my bra, letting it pop off and fly to the carpet. I shimmied out of my jeans and panties and pushed her bedroom door open.

She was on the bed, holding her phone, and I could hear Kim's voice recounting the discovery of the tell-tale heart underwear. "Maybe you should rethink the hearts on your underwear," Gemma said. "They seem to get you into trouble."

I slid onto the bed beside her, watching myself on screen going down on Kim. "I don't need them anymore." I tugged her—*my*—panties over her hips and pulled them off. "I found the ones I lost."

She tossed the phone aside and pulled me to her, grabbing my face and kissing me with a furious passion. "I've been going crazy thinking about this," she said. "It's taken every fiber of strength to keep my hands off you—and myself—while you've been telling me your tales."

The phone on the bed broadcast the sounds of my moans when Pete entered me from behind. "Well, now, you have me. You can do whatever you want."

She moaned as I rubbed the mound between her legs, pressing it with my palm, teasing her lips with my fingers.

She reached down and spread her lips apart with her index finger and thumb. Her middle finger pushed on mine, and then they were both inside her. She moaned again. I let her manipulate my hand as I kissed her neck, sucking on her tender skin, working my way down her chest. I took each nipple in my teeth and bit down just enough to elicit a squeal from her, then I dragged my tongue across her ribs, letting my free hand wander to her breasts.

As my head passed over her belly button, I pivoted and swung one leg over her, so now I was straddling her, inverted, kissing her below the waist. If she weren't waxed clean, I'd be nose-deep in her pubic hair. She withdrew her hand, dragging her fingers over my face. I smelled her musk and felt the familiar quickening surge through me. After what amounted to a week of foreplay, I couldn't believe I was about to eat her out.

My tongue darted along her slit, lapping up her juices. I knew I was getting just as wet, and when her tongue began probing my pussy, I cried out. She wrapped her arms around my waist and pulled me down tight to her mouth. Her fingers were in and out of me, her tongue doing figure eights around my clit, through my labia, and back. We were devouring each other, our mouths hungry and searching, our tongues insistent, our hands and fingers seemingly everywhere.

Over our moans, the video on the phone reached the crescendo where Kim, Pete, and I all came at once, all of us screaming with feral pleasure. Gemma bucked her hips up, and I felt a gush of her juices. I pressed my face tight against her and let her cum in my mouth. She convulsed under me, moaning her pleasure into my pussy, and the vibrations hit me just right. I fell off the wave, squirting her with my cum, my hips matching hers in an epileptic frenzy as we both came, and came again.

I collapsed, my head plopping between her legs, my breasts pressed into her stomach, and hers into mine, my pussy resting against her chin. The video on the phone was at the point where I was being kicked out of Kim's house. I felt Gemma reach for it, and a second later, the sound was gone.

"Holy shit," Gemma said and laughed. She was claiming Kim's catch phrase, and I was okay with that.

"I've heard that a lot lately. I must be doing something right."

She kissed the inside of my right thigh. "Damn right, you are. There's just one problem."

I lifted my head. "What's that?"

"I'm gonna want it again in a few minutes."

I pushed myself up and flipped, so I lay beside her. Our breasts touched, and I felt a spark run through me. "I don't think that's going to be an issue."

She kissed me again, and we could taste each other's juices. She threw a leg over me, pulling our hips together, and for the remainder of the night, we were glued to each other, one being, riding wave after wave of pleasure, until we passed out, physically spent, emotionally fulfilled, and happier than either of us had been in a long time.

Darcy and Gemma will return in *Candid Camera*

If you enjoyed this tale, please leave a review. If you didn't, please forget I said anything.

About The Author

HA Blackwood:

- Is a project manager by day and author by night
- Lives in beautiful northern Colorado
- Takes orders from a three-year-old beagle
- Can't wait to release the next book featuring Darcy Ford and Gemma Amante
- Thinks the best way to eat a Kit-Kat is right out of the refrigerator
- Is a runner, but could not keep up with either Darcy or Gemma
- Is on Facebook: facebook.com/HABlackwood
- Is on Twitter: @HABlackwood7